Antoinette and Her Friends Resist

Antoinette and Her Friends Resist

Stephanie C. Fox

QueenBeeBooks

Bloomfield, Connecticut, U.S.A.

Library of Congress Cataloging-in-Publication Data
Name: Fox, Stephanie C., author.
Title: Antoinette and Her Friends Resist / Stephanie C. Fox.
Description: Connecticut: QueenBeeBooks [2025].
Identifiers: ISBN 978-1-7343743-3-9 (paperback)
Subjects: 1. Fiction—Feminist. 2. Fiction—Political. 3.
Crafts & Hobbies—Dolls & Doll Clothing.

www.queenbeeedit.com

Cover design by Stephanie C. Fox
Images created by Stephanie C. Fox
Dolls and their clothes by Stephanie C. Fox
Printed in the United States of America

Other Books by Stephanie C. Fox:

Antoinette: A Year in the Life of a Doll with Her Friends

Nae-Née – Birth Control: Infallible, with Nanites and Convenience for All

Vaccine: The Cull – Nae-Née Wasn't Enough

New World Order Underwater – The Nae-Née Inventors Strike Back

*The Book of Thieves
The Bear Guarding the Beehive*

Scheherazade Cat: The Story of a War Hero

An American Woman in Kuwait

Hawai'i – Stolen Paradise: A Travelogue

Hawai'i – Stolen Paradise: A Brief History

The Visitor Experience at the Mark Twain House

The Slamming Door: Bone Cancer, Asperger's, and Loss

Elephant's Kitchen – An Aspergirl's Study in Difference

Almost a Meal – A True Tale of Horror

The characters and events in this book are fictitious.

Any similarity to persons living or dead is purely
coincidental.

Dolls represent us.
They do what we want to do.
Perhaps they can show us how to make a
better world a reality.

This book is for people who care about democracy.

That means protecting female bodily autonomy.

We must all work to beat back fascism and misogyny if we hope to have a healthy political system, civil society, economy, and ecosystem.

For independent women.

Table of Contents

The Situation

Antoinette was angry, and she had a plan.

She wouldn't bury the lede: women were dying.

The law had been weaponized against them to take away reproductive rights and access to the reproductive healthcare that goes with that, particularly abortion.

Actually, Antoinette was furious.

She had plenty of company, both with her friends and with complete strangers around the planet.

This was the situation:

The previous November, Antoinette had given a concert on Election Day. It dealt with a crucial national question: would we come out of the polls with a woman who worked all her life as an attorney and a politician to uphold democracy and help others, or would a bully return to the White House?

The bully had won.

Antoinette had coined a name for him: Herr Pumpkingropenfuhrer.

This moniker covered his fascist tendencies, his orange visage, and his criminal dealings with women.

That was just the beginning of the explanation for Antoinette's anger, because it wasn't simply that the candidate she had voted for hadn't won the election. It was much worse than that.

The bully was making this a revenge presidency.

There were currently more than 8.2 billion people living on the Earth. That was a lot of people to either get along with or offend, to help or hurt.

Hurting people is never productive for anyone.

Herr Pumpkingropenfuhrer was breaking laws, ignoring laws, and ordering the prosecution of anyone who had ever challenged him, both personally and during his previous term.

This time, he had staffed his administration with like-minded sycophants who consistently flattered him and did his bidding.

That meant doing things that, for the attorneys, would have gotten them disbarred in a properly functioning democracy. For all them, it could have meant prison.

They were religious nationalist fascists, and their isolationist policies had already racked up a huge national debt in just a few months.

Meanwhile, taking advantage of the groundwork laid during the bully's previous presidency, state attorneys general and legislators were waging war on women's reproductive health.

Many state legislatures had banned abortion at every stage of pregnancy, including before a woman could know that she was pregnant. They were criminalizing miscarriages, surveilling women and their physicians, and prosecuting them.

Antoinette wasn't alone with her fury; with her friends, Lilith, Ileandra, Manon, Mallory, Jasvinder, Nichelle, and Willow, they were eight dolls.

They were angry that a selfish, obtuse, and deliberately stupid bully was back to do as much damage he could. He was assiduously breaking the institutions of government.

That bully had been voted out of office after one term, and four years of competent leadership and respect for democracy had ensued.

Another politician -a decent man with a law degree – had worked to undo the damage he had done to our nation's standing in the international community, to our environmental laws, and our sense of democracy and the rule of law.

But the bully, after spending those intervening years being prosecuted for crimes and fraud, and convicted of rape in a civil court, was voted back in.

He had lied to the voters, promising to "only be a dictator for a day." Enough of them believed him to vote him back into office.

Dictators never revert to being democratic, no matter what they say otherwise, but enough voters had fallen for it to vote him back into office.

Herr Pumpkingropenfuhrer had a colossal sense of entitlement, he cared only for his own self-aggrandizement, and he displayed signs of dementia.

He scolded any journalist who dared to challenge him with a question, then banned them from government premises.

He couldn't abide the slightest criticism from anyone, not even late-night comedians. He was the equivalent of a king who could neither cope with nor accept jokes from a court jester.

He ignored his oath to uphold and defend the Constitution of the United States.

In short, Herr Pumpkingropenfuhrer was a fascist dictator, and he was doing his best to murder democracy in the United States of America.

The fascists had a slogan that was worn on red caps, tee shirts, and emblazoned on signs and bumper stickers:

Make America Great Again.

But America was already great, just not in their view. America was a melting pot of people, cultures, cuisines, skills, etc.

The fascist slogan needed a slight revision:

Make America Grate Again.

The credit for that quip went to Antoinette's father, with whom she watched MSNBC and CNN's news reports with disgust.

Liberty, justice, equality…it was getting more and more inclusive of all citizens, so that people of all races, creeds, backgrounds, of both sexes, and whatever sexual preference would have access to education, work, and other opportunities.

Many white males saw their group's dominance in the nation shrinking as other people gained access, and they were angry. They wanted to roll the clock back on all that.

So, one of them wrote Agenda 2025, named for the year that the orange fascist was projected to return to power for a second term as president of the United States.

Agenda 2025 attacks liberal intellectual academic policies, voting rights, reproductive rights, access to books and other written material that wasn't in line with fascism and authoritarianism: gay rights in art and entertainment, transgender people in the military, women in the military, and many other things exhibited by a diverse, free, civil society.

To enforce this, the author of Agenda 2025 had been put in charge of handling the nation's budget.

The nation was as divided, as it had been before the Civil War of 1861-1865. That division had been about slavery. The current conflict was between those who wanted democracy and those who felt overlooked by it.

Antoinette, meanwhile, has realized that she was not powerless to fight back. She was personally wealthy, and had not tied up all of her money in the stock market, or even the bulk of it. It was available for a fight, and with her friends, she was well-equipped and determined to resist.

The Dolls

This is Antoinette.

Antoinette is a virtuoso concert violinist, a composer, a conductor, and a soprano opera singer who graduated from the Julliard School of Music in New York City. She also studied at the Curtis School of Music in Philadelphia, Pennsylvania.

Her violin was made by luthier Antonio Stradivarius in the 1680s.

Antoinette keeps smiling, ready to please her listeners. Because she is on the autism spectrum, she does not always make eye contact. Nevertheless, she makes sure to do that when she is done speaking, singing, or playing.

She has an extensive wardrobe, as her profession necessitates attention to sartorial details. Her couturière is happy to make her dresses and other outfits. Stephanie C. Fox designs and sews everything for Antoinette and her friends – and with pockets, because women's clothing should always have them.

Antoinette gives concerts around the United States and in other nations. Her concerts often have a theme: herstory (women's history!), ecosystems and environmental protection, holidays, politics and current events.

She divides her personal time between Avon, Connecticut, where she has a house near her family, and New York City, where she has an apartment.

Her net worth, which is over $40 million, has taken on an importance beyond that of simply taking care of herself and those she loves, because Antoinette has made up her mind to fight fascism – particularly over women's reproductive autonomy.

She will be funding a resistance effort that shall include the participation of her friends.

They are looking forward to it.

Lilith Hermione Wandcraft, Esquire

This is Lilith Hermione Wandcraft.

Lilith is a witch, a lawyer, and a politician.
She grew up in Washington, D.C. and New York
City. Lilith graduated from New York University and
the Georgetown University Law Center.
She has a concerned expression because she has
plenty to be worried about.

Lilith just left a post that ended with the election of a fascist president.

For 4 years, she worked for a decent, law-respecting, democratic-minded president of the United States, as a member of the Cabinet, in a secret post: Secretary of Magic. She carried sensitive and top-secret documents that required a secure transport.

She also met with her counterparts at state and local levels at home, and internationally.

Lilith enjoyed that job because it gave her a chance to make a difference in the world.

All that is over now, and although it is normal in the United States for the personnel of a presidential administration to be replaced when a new one is elected, what is happening now is not.

Therefore, Lilith will be working with her close friend Antoinette to help resist the radical fascist takeover of her country.

The dolls will need Lilith's legal advice in order to carry out their plan to maintain female bodily autonomy in the face of a pandemic of anti-abortion policies.

It's a legal hellscape, and Lilith is determined to fight it.

Ileandra

This is Ileandra.

Ileandra is a botanist from a planet that is light-years away from Earth, elsewhere in our Milky Way galaxy.

Don't ask me her middle or last name. They are too difficult for a human to pronounce, and she hasn't spelled either one for me.

Ileandra's huge eyes evolved due to a nocturnal work pattern. Her planet's ecosystem is severely depleted. Millennia ago, its climate changed drastically due to overconsumption of resources, making most regions very hot – too hot to work outside during the day.

Because that damage was inflicted millennia ago, by her people's ancestors, few plants and insects thrive there. Food is scarce. And it is too hot to work outside during the day.

Ileandra has traveled to our planet to collect samples of as many plants as she can, to take them home with her. She will then work to make them thrive in greenhouses and ultimately outside, in the ecosystem, to provide more nutritious food for her people to eat.

Ileandra has visited Antoinette and Lilith before, and she is back to collect more plants.

Her favorite fruit, after all that she has found on Earth, is still the strawberry, though she is always ready to try others.

Ileandra is very interested in the people of Earth, because they are following the same self-destructive pattern that her own people did eons ago. It is sad to watch, but she can't stop herself from doing so.

Watching it all feels like watching a slow-moving vehicle crash with devastating, maiming injuries.

Mallory Miranda Moonmist, M.D.

This is Mallory.

Mallory is a witch and a gynecologist.
Mallory grew up in Salem, Massachusetts, and
met Lilith each summer from age 10 through high
school as they attended the Salem School for
Witchcraft, which was a summer program there.

Mallory's favorite subject in witch school was potions, while Lilith preferred fighting the dark arts – fitting choices considering their future non-magic professions!

Because Lilith was not from the area, she would stay with Mallory and her family each summer, thus ingraining a life-long friendship.

Later, Mallory did her pre-medical studies (with minors in political science and women's studies) at Columbia University. Antoinette met her eating lunch at a Le Pain Quotidien, was introduced to Lilith later on, and from there, their friendships grew.

At Harvard Medical School, Mallory knew she wanted to become a gynecologist. She worked hard and on matching day, which is when soon-to-be-graduates find out where they will do their residencies, she found out that she would be at the Brigham and Women's Hospital next.

From there, she decided that home is best, and joined a medical practice in the Boston area. Eventually, she established her own practice in Salem, Massachusetts, and she donates her services to migrant women and low-income women.

No one should have to live with ruined health or a forced pregnancy – or die – due a law that dictates that. This situation arose in the past few years, due to the orange fascist. Mallory came of age with the ruling of *Roe v. Wade* in place, and now it is gone.

Mallory is able to deliver a proper standard of care to her local patients, but she is not satisfied with that. What about women in other states?!

This is Manon.

Manon is an art historian and curator.
Manon is Belgian and French; her father grows
pears in the Flemish Brabant region of Belgium, and
her mother is from Paris, France. She grew up
traveling between both places, enjoying all that each
has to offer in art and culture.

She is a graduate of the Sorbonne in Paris, where she studied art history and ancient texts. She surprised her family after that by announcing her intention to study in the United States, where she completed her M.A. in Museum Studies, History Track, at Cooperstown, New York, followed by a Ph.D. in Preservation Studies at The Winterthur/University of Delaware.

She divides her time between Paris and New York City, working at the Louvre and Christie's Auction House.

Manon has had an H-1B visa to work in the United States for many years. It is for specialty occupations, which includes work as a curator.

However, she is applying for permanent United States citizenship. She can do that without giving up her French and Belgian citizenships. This is more about personal and employment security than love of America, unfortunately.

If America were still functioning as a healthy democracy, Manon would be looking forward to being a member of that as well, but instead, she is focused more on protecting herself. If she has any healthcare needs that feel threatened or insecure, she will go back to France to deal with them.

Manon has an American fiancé from whom she does not want to be blocked by any isolationist political agenda. He works as a restaurateur, running his own French-Indian fusion establishment in Manhattan. He is applying for French citizenship so he can open a location in Paris.

This is Jasvinder.

Jasvinder is an internationally acclaimed sitar player and singer.
She is from India, and she appears in many Bollywood movies, so she lives in Mumbai.

However, she travels internationally to give concerts, which is how she met Antoinette.

They first met during a term at the Juilliard School in New York City, where they participated in some group performances. This is a crucial part of the musical education offered at the Juilliard School.

Jasvinder has studied the sitar in India with the renowned Anoushka Shankar at the Shankar Mahadevan Academy and the Madras Music Academy before going to work as a professional sitarist.

She lives with her family and enjoys cooking traditional Indian foods, including Hindu and Sikh cuisine favorites with her sister, who is a practitioner of Ayurvedic medicine.

When she is not away giving concerts or practicing on her sitar, Jasvinder loves to go with her sister to shop for spices, mangoes, and other fresh ingredients.

The family garden is full of herbs and her favorite flowers, jasmine and lotus. The lotus is the national flower of India, and it grows in a small pond in their yard – mostly white and pink.

Jasvinder is very politically aware and well-informed. She is concerned about climate change, as the increase in temperatures is felt with particular intensity in her country.

Another issue that concerns her deeply is human overpopulation, a thing that she has in common with Antoinette. India's population has surpassed that of China recently, and is currently at 1.4 billion…the highest count of any nation on Earth.

Nichelle Ida Belle, D.V.M., Ph.D.

This is Nichelle.

Nichelle is a veterinary marine biologist.
She grew up in New Orleans, Louisiana, where
she graduated from the prestigious Catholic school
for Black girls, St. Mary's Academy. She was then
accepted to college and graduate school at Tulane
University, where she ended up on the faculty. This
fit in perfectly with her career plans and intention of
remaining near her family.

However, for veterinary school, she had to leave the state. She graduated from the University of Florida's College of Veterinary Medicine in Gainesville, which offers the chance to do clinical work with stranded marine life.

Nichelle loves living in New Orleans for several reasons: the Creole and Cajun food, the music and Mardi Gras festivals, the history and historic sites of the city, and the warm climate. She hates the cold. Her small apartment is located in the French Quarter, with a balcony overlooking the street.

Her work as a professor of ecology and evolutionary biology keeps her busy traveling whenever she is not teaching. A typical academic year has her teaching a cohort of graduate students who are working toward doctorates in marine biology while giving lectures and visiting aquariums.

Nichelle tends to think of aquariums as marine creature prisons. Nevertheless, she visits the inmates to provide them with veterinary care, graduate students in tow.

During the summer months, Nichelle will go out on her research boat, the *Yemoja*, with several of her graduate students. She likes to scuba dive in the Caribbean Sea and look for sea turtles. Plastic pollution is an ever-present health risk to marine life, and she tries to help the turtles as often as she can.

She loves other sea and aquatic creatures, particularly otters, but she doesn't have to go out to sea to find them. They prefer the estuary of the Mississippi River, including Lake Pontchartrain.

Willow Ophelie Noyer, C.P.A.

This is Willow.

    Willow is an accountant and art history enthusiast.

    She is Québécoise. That means that she is Canadian, a native French speaker, and that she is from the province of Québéc.

    She grew up in Québéc City, in the Frontenac Hotel, which looks a lot like a French chateau. It dominates the city skyline, towering over the historic district from a hill that overlooks the city.

Willow had the run of that hotel as a child, watching the guests. She loved listening to them interact with each other, and hearing them describe their travels and careers. It made her realize that she didn't want to be a hotelier, like her parents.

Willow attended the prestigious McGill University in Montreal, where she majored in accounting and art history. Known as Canada's Cultural Capital, that city was a wonderful place for an art lover, with an annual fireworks festival, a symphony orchestra, and several film festivals.

After that, she went to Providence, Rhode Island for her training as a travel agent, where she enjoyed visiting the art museum at the Rhode Island School of Design. She graduated from Johnson & Wales University with an M.S. in Economic and Sustainable Global Tourism Development.

With her credentials, Willow found work as a travel agent for a company that focuses on garden tourism, called Friendship Tours, in central Connecticut.

It was after a concert that Willow attended in the Sunken Garden of the Hill–Stead Museum in Farmington, Connecticut that she met Antoinette. They chatted, and Antoinette found out that Willow was ready for another challenge: that of overseeing the logistics of her travels while managing her finances.

She was hired on the spot, and the two have been enjoying working together ever since.

Follow Antoinette and her friends as they covertly resist fascism and help other women to live as independently as they do.

Plans and Plots

Antoinette Calls a Meeting

All day, as she practiced a concerto on her violin, Antoinette thought about how she could fight back against the assault on democracy in her country.

It was a warm day in late spring, and she was enjoying practicing with the windows open in her living room in Avon, Connecticut. She sat at the back of the house, looking out at her flower garden.

She knew she couldn't work on every problem.

She went out into her garden to think, bringing her violin with her. She kept playing the concerto.

Immigration? The Alligator Auschwitz in the Everglades of Florida?!

Every day, families were being separated by masked agents from ICE – Immigration and Customs Enforcement – as parents were being kidnapped under the orange monster's orders and thrown into detention facilities…and then shipped off to prisons in countries other than their own, due process and risk of torture be damned.

Book banning?

Self-appointed bullies were pressuring librarians and teachers to not teach from books that they didn't like. Books by Black people, books by LGBTQ+ people, books by autistic people…the list of books to be excluded went on and on.

Conservation and environmental protection?

National parks and sacred native lands were under imminent threat of being sold off to corporations that wanted to mine them for minerals and fossil fuels.

Pollution emissions limits were being loosened and deregulated, rolling back the work of presidents who had cared enough to safeguard the ecosystem.

Releasing the client list of wealthy pedophiles?

The keeper of that list had died by hanging in a New York City jail under suspicious circumstances, during a few minutes in which the surveillance cameras had been shut off.

Which issue would it be, Antoinette wondered?

She would have to choose the one that bothered her most and focus on that…a favorite issue…

Women were dying or having their reproductive and other health ruined due to attacks on the right to an abortion.

That was the one – that issue was it.

It was time to make some calls.

Antoinette put her violin and bow in their case, picked up her cell phone, and scrolled through her contacts list.

She knew who she needed to involve: her friend Lilith, who was an attorney and former cabinet member to the president of the United States – the president before Herr Pumpkingropenfuhrer.

Lilith had been Secretary of Magic. She had helped out as a courier of secure documents, and whatever else the former president needed.

That president was a good, decent person, another lawyer, and one who respected and even loved the rule of law.

Antoinette had played for him and his First Lady.

But now that the fascist was in the Oval Office, Lilith was on her own. Lilith had absolutely no intention of telling HIM what she could do, let alone offering her services to him and his gang of television twits, painted patriarchal women, and podcasting creeps.

Lately, Lilith had been working with various nonprofit groups as they struggled to preserve a sense of normalcy until this was over.

Antoinette hoped that her friend would know some more people who could help make her ideas a reality.

If experience was a guide, she would.

Lilith answered her phone on the first ring.

When she heard Antoinette propose to form her own nonprofit group, she said she would come to visit the next day. "I'll bring someone with me. She's a witch, and a gynecologist. We know each other from magic school."

"Great!" Antoinette said. "That's perfect!"

Intrigued, Lilith held her questions for the visit.

Antoinette called Willow, her accountant, next.

Willow also served as her agent, arranging travel and logistics for each concert. Therefore, she lived as Antoinette did, with a place in New York City and a place in Connecticut.

Willow was in Connecticut now, with her husband, who was a writer for the Associated Press.

Yes, Willow would be at that meeting.

She was looking forward to getting acquainted with whoever else would be there, and would invite a scientist who was visiting from Louisiana.

Good.

So…who else to call?

Manon.

Manon was a curator with Christie's auction house in New York City…and also at the Louvre in Paris, France, where she was from. She divided her time between both cities.

Manon had a fiancé who also worked at Christie's. He was an American, so she was in the process of applying for U.S. citizenship. She would, of course, retain her French and Belgian citizenships, but having American documents would save her a vast amount of hassle.

It would also make her relationship fairly free from worry about being able to live with her soon-to-be husband in either country.

Antoinette didn't blame her; she herself had dual French and American citizenship, so she and her boyfriend were taking things a bit slower.

Manon was intrigued when she heard a little bit about Antoinette's plan. "You can tell me the rest in person," she said. "We don't want to share it with AI bots. And I may be able to bring some donors in."

"That's for sure," Antoinette said. "Thanks!"

They ended the call.

Who else?

For that, there would have to be introductions.

Jasvinder Frets

Jasvinder was preoccupied.

She had practiced ragas on her sitar all day, and would soon leave for a series of concerts in the United States.

She adjusted the frets of her sitar, thinking about the difficulties of moving around the world — difficulties and complications that hadn't existed before the United States had a fascist president.

Jasvinder suddenly realized that she was fretting in more ways than one, and laughed mirthlessly.

She was Indian, so her passport was from India. She was there now, practicing at home.

She knew that Willow would handle all of the logistics, planning and arranging it all, but she dreaded the actual trip.

It didn't used to be like that.

Jasvinder remembered what it was like over a decade ago, as she was finishing up a term in New York City at the Julliard School, where she and Antoinette had met, and then after that, going to and from the United States for concerts.

It used to be easy.

Just make arrangements, go on the trip, and return. No problem. No worries.

Now she had to worry about interviews each and every time she traveled.

What a nuisance!

Herr Pumpkingropenfuhrer, as Antoinette called him, had decided to make travel extremely difficult for anyone from a nation that wasn't in Europe. All this trouble to keep immigrants from entering the United States, and to punish anyone who stayed a nanosecond past their visa.

This should be a fun trip in which she played her sitar, met interesting and nice people, and then came home and told her parents and sister about it all.

Now it was a stressful experience.

Would she get grabbed by masked agents either upon arrival or during her trip, lose her sitar in the scuffle (it was finely crafted and valuable!), and end up trapped in some horror of an American concentration camp for weeks on end?!

Her fiancé had already expressed trepidation about her upcoming trip, but she wanted to see Antoinette, and she didn't want to live in fear.

She was leaving for Connecticut tomorrow; she and Antoinette had some concerts booked together.

She should be happily looking forward to this instead of feeling anxious.

Someone was rotten to the core in the United States, something religious and nationalist.

She could relate; India had a similar problem.

But that was becoming more and more common around the world as populations increased and resources were scarcer.

Her entry to the United States promised to be inconvenient, slow, and an incarceration risk just for entering while not white.

It was all so unreasonable.

It made her angry.

Antoinette would be checking in with the airport officials just to vouch for Jasvinder's right to be in the country and give sitar concerts.

No wonder her friend called that moronic orange fascist "Herr Pumpkingropenfuhrer." That moniker was just so apt.

She put the sitar down and reached out to pet Sita, her cat, who was sitting up in her bed, which was on Jasvinder's bed.

The cat purred and smiled, which made her human feel a little calmer.

Her phone rang.

It was Antoinette.

"When you get here, you will find some changes," her friend told her. "Some, you and Willow have been preparing for. Others, I will tell you about."

"Others…" Jasvinder said. "Any hints?"

"Well…I'll tell you about it all in person. That would be wiser," Antoinette hedged.

"I understand. Until then."

They said good-bye and ended the call.

Smiling, she went downstairs to eat dinner with her family.

Nichelle Leads a Field Trip

Nichelle was on her way to teach a class.

It had been raining, and she was running from the parking lot to the building across campus, trying to avoid getting too wet. It wouldn't be good to arrive looking a mess when she had a lecture to give.

Fortunately, it soon tapered off to a sprinkle and she went inside, her thoughts going back to the content of her lecture, and to summer plans to be out on the Gulf of Mexico with her graduate students, working among the sea creatures and studying the effects of pollution on their health.

Then her mind wandered some more, as she hung up her raincoat in her office.

There was a message from her friend Lilith, who helped her with obtaining grants, asking her to call. She would do that after lunch.

Would she lose funding for her projects? The current governmental administration was stripping funding for scientific research. America was going to be less competitive in the world as a result.

And scientists like Nichelle were going to lose the ability to pursue important research.

The message was not about grants, it had said.

Nichelle studied the effects of climate change and pollution on the health of marine life. Publishing her findings was a crucial part of the job. But without the funding to gather the data – including the funding to go out in the field all summer and see this damage up close and in person – it was all at risk.

She watched MSNBC and CBS's news magazine show, *60 Minutes*. She did that to keep track of what was going on. It was depressing, but necessary.

She didn't want to give Nielsen ratings to Fox News, but she felt the need to check on it sometimes, just to see what was said. That was routinely unsettling, and the routine part of it was even more so. The participants and commentators on it reveled in getting rid of Diversity, Inclusion, and Equity (DEI) hires in favor of white people...and males.

It made Nichelle angry, of course. She was hired on her merits and deserved everything she had gotten.

She would not leave. If she had to seek private donors to keep going, she would.

She had already contacted Melinda French Gates, and received a favorable response. That meant that one of her grants was safe for another five years.

She was still waiting to hear back from the ARCS Foundation, which stood for Achievement Rewards for College Scientists. It provided funding for her graduate students, who needed the funds for their research. Doctoral degrees in the sciences required lots of resources in order to complete them.

Nichelle checked her notes, then went down the hall to deliver a lecture. It was to be a short one, because she was going to take her students on a field trip today. She would explain the trip in that short lecture, and then they would leave.

She wanted her students to visit the New Orleans Flooded House Museum. It had opened in 2018, and was run by Levees.org. Artists had created the appearance of a flooded New Orleans home as it looked when city residents returned to see the devastation caused by Hurricane Katrina in 2005.

The place didn't have real mold, but otherwise it looked authentic, thanks to the skills of the artists. Authentic smells, however, would have posed health risks that would have nixed the project. You can't have everything, Nichelle thought, but this was pretty good.

Her class included twenty students. She spoke to them for about five minutes.

"Part of understanding the health of marine life is understanding the ecosystem in which these creatures live. We live in it, too, and are responsible as a species for the changing conditions of our planet's climate and weather, and what that does to habitats, including our own."

"Part of the reason why I want you to see the Flooded House Museum is that, as scientists, we often think in an emotionally detached, intellectualized way about what our species does to change and damage the ecosystem and the habitats that many nonhuman species live in…until it affects our own species."

"Seeing what a ruined human habitat looks like, and reading the museum signs that describe it all while listening to a tour guide should be a powerful experience for all of you. Hurricane Katrina was caused by human carelessness – carelessness with engineering levees and carelessness with taking care of our planet."

A student raised her hand.

"Yes – Melina."

Melina was from California. She asked, "Professor, is it true that you were here during Hurricane Katrina?"

Nichelle was glad she had asked.

"Yes, it's true. I grew up here. My parents and siblings and I lived – still live – in the French Quarter, but my grandmother lived in the Ninth Ward. Her house was completely destroyed. We got her out of there in time, though, and she came to live with us. It took us hours to drive out of the city, to Baton Rouge, but we were lucky to have started driving early."

She paused. "Anyone else have a question? No? Let's go, then."

With that, they all got up and left the lecture hall.
The sun had come out. Everything outside was still
damp or soaked through, but the weather forecast
was for sunshine the rest of the day.

The Flooded House Museum was at 5000
Warrington Drive, New Orleans, Louisiana 70122.

Visitors are allowed to walk up to it and peer into
the windows, but not to go inside.

It had first been photographed as a New Orleans
home would have looked an issue of *The Times-
Picayune* on the coffee table warning of the
hurricane's imminent arrival: "Katrina Takes Aim"
was the headline.

After that, the artists had moved in and spray-
painted stuffed animals to look waterlogged,
smashed a front leg off of a wooden piano and
painted it an awful gray, and painted the walls to
show how high the water had risen.

The water line was higher than that of a tall
human, about six feet up from the floor.

One side of the house was left gutted, showing
the wood frames of walls with the sheetrock
removed. This is done to get rid of anything that
could retain mold.

Nichelle remembered the horrid stench left by
the damage, and shared her memories with the class.
Even the tour guide looked unsettled.

"I can never forget that smell," Nichelle said. "It
was a nauseating mix of rot: mold, mildew, bodies,
sewage, trash, ruined food, and soaked building
materials."

A yellow "X" was marked on the brick by the front door, with other things around it. One line of it as the rescuers from out of state entered, and the other after they came out. The date went on top: "9/22" for September 22, 2005. To the left it said "Pa" for Pennsylvania.

This house didn't have other markings, but there were codes for the right side to indicate problems such as rats or mold. The bottom of the "X" said "0" to indicate that no one, living or dead, had been found inside.

On the ride back to the University, Nichelle took them to a real flooded house, one that hadn't been restored. The students were, as Nichelle had hoped, properly sobered and thoughtful from viewing and hearing it all.

Later in the day, she would work with her five graduate students in the laboratory, and plan their summer on the *Yemoja*, her research boat.

A Friend Returns

Antoinette went into her kitchen and started making dinner.

She found lots of fresh vegetables – tomatoes, Vidalia onion, garlic, a jalapeño pepper, yellow bell peppers, cucumbers – and put them in the blender to make gazpacho. After seeding the tomatoes and cucumbers, added salt and freshly ground pepper, several ice cubes, she put the lid on and made a purée of it all.

Her fiancé was teaching at the University of Hartford as a visiting professor, so they were both spending a lot more time in Connecticut lately than usual.

Not that they didn't keep going back to Manhattan, what with his job at the Museum of Natural History, but this was what their schedule would look like for the next year.

Her fiancé arrived, kissed her, and looked happily at the gazpacho.

He was feeling ambitious, so he took out rainbow carrots, a red onion, garlic, and jalapeno and Fresno peppers, too. Antoinette watched happily as he made basmati rice and a fragrant, delicious carrot curry.

Antionette had made lavender honey ice cream.

After a pleasant meal, the two of them settled onto the living room sofa to watch *Real Time with Bill Maher* and *Last Week Tonight* with John Oliver.

Stephen Colbert was off; it was a Friday night.

At half past midnight, they had seen enough TV.

They got up, and Antoinette reached out to pet her cat, Specter the Spectator. He was watching their every move, waiting until bedtime.

The cat jumped down from his favorite chair and followed them as they walked around the room, turning things off for the night.

Specter moved to the window at the back of the room, which overlooked the backyard garden. He started washing his tail. Suddenly, though, he sat up, wide-eyed and startled.

At the same time, Antoinette and her fiancé heard something out there.

There was a brief flash of light, and then nothing.

But the cat was now staring steadily out at the night with rapt attention.

"That feels very familiar," Antoinette said, going over to the back door to look through its upper glass section.

Sure enough, someone she knew was out there.

Ileandra had come back to visit her again.

Like a seasoned interstellar traveler with a destination in mind, the alien was carrying her environmental suit in her gray kit bag, walking across the lawn toward the back door.

When the cat saw her come up to the door, he relaxed and settled down. He remembered her.

Antoinette yanked the back door open and hugged her friend.

"You're back! You came back! I thought you would never visit again!"

She was grinning from ear to ear, delighted.

Ileandra was thrilled, too. "Yes, I'm back. I came to visit you on purpose this time, not by accident, and to stay a while and gather more Earth foods."

She hugged Antoinette back, put her bag and suit down, and reached out to pet the cat.

"It's nice to see you again, Specter," she told him telepathically.

He narrowed his eyes in a cat smile and purred.

Antoinette's fiancé smiled and nodded to the alien, and everyone, including the cat, went upstairs for the night.

Manon Arrives

Antoinette and Ileandra waited until mid-morning, and then got into Antoinette's car to go into Hartford.

Ileandra had a new dress already.

"It was left here somehow after your previous visit," Antoinette had told her. "You never got to wear it, so at least you have one outfit here…other than your blue work clothes," she said with a grin.

They parked at the train station, went in, and met Manon on the platform.

Manon would be staying for the weekend, and the three of them would go back to New York City together on Monday.

"So," Manon said, alighting from the train, "are you going to tell me what you're planning in the car? And introduce me?" she added, smiling at Ileandra. She looked at her curiously.

There weren't a lot of people around, but they headed outside quickly to Antoinette's car as they spoke.

"Yes," Antoinette said, clicking the remote-control key to open the doors. "To begin with, this is my friend Ileandra. She is a botanist. She arrived last night. And…" here Antoinette paused for dramatic effect, "…Ileandra is from another planet, in a faraway solar system."

Manon stared at the two of them like she had heard wrong.

Then she looked carefully at Ileandra.

After a moment, she nodded. "I can see the slight differences now that you tell me that. Have you visited Earth before?"

They settled into their seats and buckled their seat belts.

Ileandra nodded. "Yes, many times. But this is my second visit with Antoinette. The first one was by accident; I got left behind when some people near Antoinette's neighborhood surprised our team – of three – in the middle of the night."

Antoinette added with a grin, "I found her the next morning in my garden with an uprooted strawberry plant."

Manon shook her head. "This is amazing! And this second visit is on purpose, I must assume."

"It is," the alien replied with a little smile.

"She came back for more plants – plants she couldn't get by skulking around at night, keeping herself hidden," Antoinette said. "I'm glad you're back," she told Ileandra. "And Lilith will be happy to see you again."

"Lilith knows Ileandra?" Manon asked.

"Yes. But that's it." Then Antoinette added, "Until now," with a grin.

Ileandra smiled. "It will be good to see Lilith again, too," she said.

Antoinette was excited.

After being angry for months, she was doing something constructive about this hostile corporate takeover of the nation by a spoiled, incompetent fascist.

It felt good…so good.

If she had anything to with it, after this meeting, she and her friends would soon feel better very often, and not just get a one-time emotional high.

Ileandra showed Manon to her room. They came back downstairs immediately, though, to help get things ready for the visitors.

They walked into the open kitchen in time to see
Antoinette take out a flourless chocolate torte with
thick, silky chocolate ganache.

"You made that, didn't you?" Manon said,
looking at the torte with a pleased smile. "How can I
help get ready?"

"I did," Antoinette said, "and you can set up the
coffee machine to brew a full pot of hazelnut
coffee." She brought out the coffee, the scoop, and
left Manon to it as she laid out lots of cups, a bowl
full of granulated brown sugar, and a pitcher of milk.

The doorbell rang.
Willow had come to the meeting.
She had arrived at the same time as Nichelle.
Antoinette greeted Willow with a grin and left her
to go get a cup of coffee; she knew her way around.

"Dr. Belle, it's lovely to meet you!" Antoinette
said, turning to meet the scientist.

"Lovely to meet you too!" Nichelle said, smiling.
"As a resident of a forced birther state, I'm so
pleased that you invited me."

Antoinette said, "Of course! You will add a perspective that we lack. Please keep what we discuss at this meeting secret."

Nichelle nodded, saying, "I promise."

Antoinette thanked her and told her to get comfortable in the living room.

Lilith was the next to arrive, with a friend, Dr. Mallory M. Moonmist, in tow.

"Mallory is a gynecologist," Lilith informed Antoinette, "and a witch. Also, although she is from a state that recognizes the right to choose whether or not to have an abortion, and works in 3 such states, she is very upset about this issue."

"Welcome," Antoinette said, delighted to hear this. "I'm thrilled to meet you! What states do you practice in?"

"Thank you for having me here. Connecticut, Massachusetts, and New York. But I want to help women in anti-abortion states before their health is ruined, and keep them from being prosecuted. Lilith has been advising me about the pitfalls of this, and on how to not get caught helping."

Antoinette grinned. "I'll bet she has. The politicians are helping with full faith and credit laws, but not fast enough. Women can't wait for them to get all that done. Health care needs don't pause while the politicians debate and dither — or block laws that support women's bodily autonomy."

"Exactly!" chorused Lilith and Mallory.

They settled themselves in the back of the house, meeting Manon, Willow, Nichelle, and Ileandra, and getting coffee.

Lilith and Ileandra had a brief and happy reunion.

"You came back to see us again!" Lilith said, hugging her.

"Yes," Ileandra said. "Of course I want more Earth plants, but I missed you! And I want to see what you are up to. I was following the political news, and it's alarming! Environmental laws are being eviscerated at the speed of light, and women are being treated as secondary to a microscopic embryo. I had to come back!"

Willow, Nichelle, and Mallory were astonished to be in the presence of an alien, but they soon adjusted to the idea, delighted by it…and her.

After a brief chat about how amazing it was to meet an alien from another planet, and a botanist at that, the group settled into the sofas to focus on the purpose of their gathering.

Antoinette got a cup of hazelnut coffee, served the torte, and sat down.

Specter jumped into a cat bed in an end table next to the sofa and sat with her, purring and watching everyone.

"What a beautiful cat!" Mallory said.

Antoinette smiled. "He's a lovely, sweet boy."

With that, Antoinette got down to business.

"Herr Pumpkingropenfuhrer can get his tiny, misogynist hands off of our bodies and keep them off," Antoinette said, kicking off their meeting.

This statement would characterize the agenda and the attitude that motivated it.

"I've been calling him OFF, because there's something really off about him," Willow said. "The nerve of the Orange Flatulent Fascist to say that 2 dolls are enough!" Willow added. "There are several of us, after all. OFF can mind his own business and just be unhappy about it!"

Laughter all around.

"So," Antoinette said, "why are we daring to do this, considering that the law, after being on our side for 50 years, suddenly is not? As if that question doesn't answer itself! But seriously: why break the laws of anti-abortion states?"

Blank stares.

"Come on, Lilith – you're a lawyer. You should know this one."

Lilith looked startled. "I suppose it's some out-of-the-box idea you have. Please just tell us."

"Okay. That's what I wanted to point out in this discussion: not all laws merit respect. Women are being denied bodily autonomy and treated by lawmakers as if we are secondary to a microscopic cluster of cells. We should not respect that."

"Okay…" Lilith said, "I can see a parallel to slavery. Abolitionists took the same view. There was no excuse for respecting the Fugitive Slave Act of 1850, so they campaigned openly for the end of it and of slavery while secretly operating the network of the Underground Railroad."

"Exactly!" Antoinette said. "So, you see my point. I just wanted someone to say that before we set up the infrastructure of our covert op."

"Hear, hear!" Mallory and Nichelle said.

"Look at all of the money these stupid bans have cost," Willow said. "People don't want to live, work, or study in states that have abortion bans."

"I certainly wouldn't move to one," Manon said.

"You work in New York and Paris anyway," Antoinette said, grinning at her. "You're safe. Maybe I should protest by refusing to give some concerts in some of these places…if asked by MAGAs."

"Good idea," Lilith said. "And why not? Seth Rogen refused to pose for a photograph with former U.S. House Speaker Paul Ryan when his kids brought him over. He was like, 'No way, man! If I do that, people will think I agree with you politically, and I don't!'"

Nichelle laughed at that. Then she said, "Well, I am from Louisiana. My whole family lives there, and has for as far back as we can remember. I won't be moving, but I am furious at the cancellation of reproductive health care services and choices. I'm worried about my female graduate students, and I'm hoping that I will find out something about how to help them, if they end up needing it."

Everyone nodded.

"We'll do the best we can to offer that."

Antoinette added, "Crisis Pregnancy Centers are a scam by anti-abortionists. Part of the mission statement of this resistance group will be to counteract their efforts."

Manon asked, "Why is this such a problem for us?!" She was just angry. It was a rhetorical question, to show her outrage and frustration. "In France, the right to abortion has been added to our Constitution just because of the trouble we saw here in the United States."

Mallory had the answer for her.

"It has always been all about controlling women. This has gone on since what was called the Burning Times. In history books, though, it is called the Dark Ages. But for women – any women, whether herbalists, who were treated as witches, or not – it was about taking health care work and control of it away, no matter the cost to our health."

Willow asked, "So burning women as witches was really about rooting out women who were health care practitioners?!"

"Yes," Mallory said. "Herbalists, midwives…all were murdered under the auspices of attacking a pre-Christian, nature-worshipping, goddess-focused religion, which we now know as Wicca. But it was also misogynist at its core, and it left one woman alive in every village."

Willow and Manon's eyes widened.

Antoinette just listened. She knew all this; she had read extensively about it.

Mallory continued, "This has been the situation for long after that, into the 19th century and up to today. Abortionists were persecuted and prosecuted relentlessly in 19th century America. The aim was to take all of women's bodily autonomy and health care, particularly reproductive health, out of women's hands. Male physicians didn't want the professional competition."

"That's why the Comstock Act of 1873 was enacted," Lilith added. "Anthony Comstock and P.T. Barnum were among the men who sought to take all agency about our bodies away from women."

"P.T. Barnum?! The circus guy?" Willow asked, aghast.

"Yeah, that was him," Antoinette confirmed. "Except that they couldn't do anything about women going to medical school. Look at Dr. Elizabeth Blackwell, for example."

"Yes – and that is what motivated me to become a gynecologist," Mallory said. "Of course, I was happy for a long time, delivering health care as a woman to women patients, with no worry, thanks to having the law as it should always be, on our side. But now it's not, so here we are, planning our work as Janes."

Willow glanced up, puzzled, but she was busy pulling files from the internet to handle the accounting of the project, and didn't ask about that reference.

'No problem,' Antoinette thought to herself. 'It'll come up later.'

She said aloud, "Liberals get a lot of criticism for working on a multitude of issues at once while democracy is on the line. But we need to do that for another reason: to keep up appearances as a distraction while focusing covertly on delivering reproductive healthcare to women all over the United States – no matter which state they live in. That means including other issues aimed at maintaining and repairing democracy in civil society."

"What do you have in mind?" Willow asked.

"Anti-book banning and data rescue efforts. Perhaps some supplies for No Kings protests. And perhaps some legal assistance for legal immigrants who are getting harassed, grabbed, detained, and otherwise made miserable by Herr Pumpkingropenfuhrer."

"We could sponsor those things," Lilith agreed. "What else do you have in mind?"

"We need to spread a strategy that will win back voters from the MAGA camp. We need to make a philosophy catch on: economic populism v. cultural populism."

Everyone glanced around, wondering what this meant.

Ileandra just watched the conversation like it was a slow-moving arrow finding its target.

She looked happy to see this, and happy to have a cup of hazelnut coffee in her hands, sniffing it and sipping it slowly. Antoinette had put a lot of coconut milk in it, hoping it wouldn't be too strong for her.

Nichelle was watching her.

She said, "You must be appalled to see that humans are in such a terrible situation."

The alien looked at her. "Yes, I am. This is what my people went through eons ago. All life was treated as sacred, until we had too many people putting too much pressure on our planet's ecosystem."

"What happened once your ancestors realized this?" Lilith asked.

"Arguments. Diplomatic breakdown. Wars."

"And when that was over, and everyone was exhausted by that – then what?" Lilith pressed.

"Then our planet was in even worse condition, and it still is. That is why I'm back here. Your planet has lots of edible plants that our people are able to eat, but we need more varieties."

"We'll get them for you," Antoinette promised.

"Thank you. Thank you very much," the alien said, smiling at her. "I – we – really appreciate it."

Mallory spoke up. "You still look anxious, even after that promise. What else is on your mind?"

Ileandra sighed. "I have another assignment…one that is outside my area of expertise. I'm worried about that other project, and have no experience going about it.

"What is it?" Willow asked.

Another deep sigh. "A xenoanthropologist found out about my previous visit and interactions with humans. She interviewed me extensively. When she was finished, I thought she would be satisfied…until she found out that I was coming back here."

"She must be so jealous that you are here," Antoinette said, as a slow grin spread across her face.

Everyone glanced at her, then back at the alien.

Ileandra nodded. "She must be. She has insisted that I write a memoir about this trip, plus my previous one, and, unfortunately for me, not just about collecting plants."

Antoinette burst out laughing.

So did Manon.

"What?" Ileandra said, sounding annoyed.

"Lots of physicians and scientists are anxious about having to write," Mallory said. "I have published some scientific articles for high-impact, peer reviewed journals, but I also have colleagues who are terrified of writing."

Nichelle nodded sympathetically. "I can relate. I was anxious about the 'publish or perish' aspect of teaching in a university, but I made myself get past it, and now I have twenty papers to show for it."

Manon chimed in. "Most of the writing I do is those little exhibit notices that go on the walls next to artwork in museums and auction houses, but I also write letters and reports on the art."

Lilith said, "Lawyers have to write all the time, but it is a specific kind of writing: briefs, pleadings, memoranda, and letters, mostly. Some of us like to write novels, though, and are quite successful at it."

Antoinette was considering all this. "I have an idea. I don't just compose music. I like to write dystopian science fiction novels. My pseudonym is Stephanie C. Fox. I can help you."

The alien looked at her, eyes wider than usual. "How can you help me?" she wanted to know.

"You need to outline your memoir. You may have to do this as your visit goes along, but what I suggest is this: keep a running list in a separate place from the book manuscript with what I like to think of as catchy chapter titles. It will serve as your outline until you are finished, and then become your table of contents. Meanwhile, write each chapter as a separate file, and put them together at the end."

"Is that how you work?"

Antoinette nodded. "It is, and it's fun. You'll see. I'll help you."

Ileandra breathed another sigh, but this time it was one of relief. "Thank you! You keep saving me!"

"Oh, I think you're saving us, too, just be being here. You are giving us renewed determination by telling us about your people's experience."

Antoinette went over to her computer, made a folder that she labeled "What the Small Gray Visitor Said," and then created some files: "Table of Contents" and "Research Notes". She opened that last one and turned to Ileandra.

"I propose that one of the things that we do is publish books. We'll use my imprint of Fox Mark Books. We shall help Ileandra write her book, and send the manuscript home with her at the end of her visit. But that's not all: we shall keep a copy of it here and publish it as a work of fiction. That way, we'll get the benefit of her wisdom for humanity."

The alien gaped at her for a moment, then said, "That's a terrific idea!"

"I'm glad you approve!" Antoinette said. "We need your permission, which was the next thing I was going to ask about."

Ileandra smiled. "So…what did you open the 'Research Notes' file for? What is it for?"

"Random ideas. It's like a dumping ground for them. That way, they will be in writing for later, when you know what you want to do with them, rather than lost in a moment."

"Oh! So many perspectives on writing…" the alien said, glancing around the room.

"Let's fill in a couple of your thoughts right now, just to get you started."

Everyone clapped and cheered Ileandra on.

"Well…" Ileandra paused, thinking for a moment. "I will not ask you to take me to your leader, because you don't have one right now. My people and I know this from watching your news broadcast that you have an autocrat with dementia. He shows the classic signs of being a malignant narcissist."

The other dolls roared with laughter.

"Yes, he does!" they chorused.

Antoinette rapidly typed all that in, grinning humorlessly as she did so. "Great! What else?"

"Uh…I'm watching you plan to fight back against an insane effort to force women to birth more humans whether they want to or not, while my people have a population policy that controls our numbers quite carefully."

Antoinette typed all that.

Willow had a question. "How does that work?"

"Only those who want to reproduce are considered for permission to do so, and even then, few actually get to do it. Our people accept this restriction because we understand the damage done to our planet and the misery of starvation and war in the past. And because we are still rehabilitating our ecosystem, tens of thousands of years later."

Antoinette added this to the file.

There was a moment of silence as everyone took in what the alien had just told them.

"That is shocking to hear, but necessary," Mallory said. "Our people need to learn more about sacrificing wants that lead to resource depletion, but I fear that they won't until that damage has been done."

Lilith agreed. "Nothing is so effective as personal experience…"

"Humans need to learn to care about what affects others than themselves if they are to survive."

Ileandra had just added one more thought, which Antoinette duly typed in. Then she clicked "Save" and turned back to the group.

"So," she said, bringing the discussion back around to the business at hand, "after that long but productive tangent, let's get back on track."

Lilith nodded. "Please tell us more about this strategy. I'm sure my boyfriend will want to research it at the Brookings Institution."

"Okay," Antoinette said, pleased. "The idea is to champion the right of the working class, in particular, and everyone other than the top one percent, to a comfortable living with enough food, clothing, and shelter, plus healthcare. That's how to take those voters back from the MAGA fascists. Our organization should be helping with that effort."

"How do we do that?" Lilith asked.

"Make them feel that non-educated people are a priority. No vocabulary that smacks of college and graduate degrees. Even as we focus on promoting economic populism over the cruel and pointless social control of cultural populism, which is what the MAGAs do, we must watch how we talk. The way I just expressed that, for example, is no good for public speeches. The public presentations by our group must reflect all this."

Lilith nodded, understanding. "So – that is what we should do for our other activities, while we focus on helping women access abortion care."

"Yes," Antoinette said.

Manon wondered aloud, "It would be interesting to know just how many people in America have degrees. If we're talking to everyone, you're right that our choice of words ought to reflect that."

One of Antoinette's interests was population data. She had the answer. "The current U.S. population is over 348 million people. Out of all that, roughly 38 percent have bachelor's degrees, and 14 percent have graduate degrees of some sort."

Willow took a calculator out of her pocket. "14 percent equals 48,580,000. That's not many people. We can't talk only to them."

Everyone nodded.

Antoinette turned to Lilith again. "Could you go over recent cases about abortion law in the United States, just to bring us all up to speed on it?"

"Sure," Lilith said. "Many states, since the travesty that is the *Dobbs v. Jackson Women's Health Organization*, 597 U.S. 215 (2022) case overturned *Roe v. Wade*, 410 U.S. 113 (1973) and *Planned Parenthood v. Casey*, 505 U.S. 833 (1992), now have laws that outlaw abortion, threatening and often ruining women's health."

She paused for a moment, then added, "So much for a fundamental right to privacy, as the *Roe v. Wade* decision guaranteed. So much for the undue burden standard when evaluating state-imposed restrictions on that right, provided by *Planned Parenthood v. Casey*."

Lilith paused for breath, then added, "Men – who don't have to worry about being trapped in a pregnancy against their will, particularly one that could go wrong and kill them – have informed me, always in a tone that suggested that I was not thinking things through, that the law needed refining anyway. What they don't have a suitable answer to – what they can't have such an answer to – is the irrefutable fact that pregnant women can't afford to wait while the law is perfected and thus have their health ruined or their lives ended."

Antoinette nodded. "No woman should have to die due to a gap in the time in which the law protects our bodily autonomy. Abortion is reproductive healthcare, and we need it to be accessible without interruption!"

Cheers all around for that.

Then she outlined the agenda of the Silphium Society. "To help women in forced birther states, which is our main interest, we will need a gynecologist, which we have," she said, smiling at Mallory, "a steady supply of abortion pills, which Mallory can access and I can pay for, and we should concentrate on cases in which women cannot travel, and doctors in their states are letting their health deteriorate to dire distress rather than risk their medical licenses."

She cautioned, "We must do that without getting caught, identified, or otherwise noticed so that we won't get sued, prosecuted, banned from forced birther states, or fined for helping women who are trapped in them."

Mallory spoke up. "I can hardly wait to start helping – covertly. The idea is to not get caught so that we can keep on doing this. I will be the one actually doing it, as the gynecologist of our group. But this will still cost a lot of money."

"That's why I am instigating and funding this effort," Antoinette said. "With Willow as our accountant and Lilith as our attorney, and you as our gynecologist, plus any other assistance that Manon and Nichelle can offer, we should be able to help a lot of women."

"Anti-abortion law does not merit respect. We shall not respect it. We shall resist it by helping women who are trapped in those states to access abortion care. And you are our secret agent. This is not some impossible mission, but we don't want your identity known."

Mallory looked excited; her eyes were fiery, like it was time to celebrate a momentous occasion which, Antoinette realized, it was.

An Apt Name…and a Legal Entity is Formed

"What should we call this organization?" Mallory asked. "How about the Gilead Resistance?"

"Nice, but that's only good for us. It will have to be something that is not too obvious about its true purpose," Lilith said. "Something people have to at least look up to understand."

"Really? I half think you're right," Antoinette said, "but would love a name such as 'The Weddington Files,' for Attorney Sarah Weddington, who argued and won the *Roe v. Wade* case."

"Well…they're going to look up everything anyway and figure out whatever name we go with," Lilith conceded.

"Let's keep thinking," Antoinette said. "We don't have to come up with the perfect, catchiest name right this second. Though I would like to get that step done…"

She trailed off, still searching for the ideal name.

"It would work best if it were a 501(c)(3) organization," Willow said, smiling.

"Yes," Antoinette agreed. "The Brookings Institution and the Heritage Foundation, both think tanks but each at different ends of the political spectrum, have that status."

Lilith nodded her approval. "Definitely."

Suddenly, Antoinette had it. "How about the Silphium Society?" she said, glancing around at everyone.

"I like it…" Mallory said, grinning.

"What is silphium?" Ileandra wanted to know.

"You of all people will want to know about it," Antoinette told her. "It's an extinct herb that the ancient Romans supposedly used as an abortifacient."

Manon and Willow were nodding, pleased with the name.

Lilith smiled and said, "Terrific! Now we can get on with the work of creating this think tank."

The Silphium Society would need a mission statement to explain its purpose.

"Lobbyists will be employed to relentlessly communicate with politicians – pro-choice, pro-abortion access politicians – about the necessity for packing the courts with judges who are friendly to the right to abortion on demand," Antoinette said.

"It's unfortunate that that is what it takes to safeguard this right, but that's the reality of it," Lilith said, nodding her agreement with this.

"That will be the overt effort," Antoinette said. "The covert one, funded by an endowment that I shall provide, will of course be to provide abortion care to women who are stuck in anti-abortion states. This will take the form of sending them medication – abortion pills – and helping them to travel to states where abortion is legal to get them. So many women who need abortions can't afford to travel, so the idea is to solve that part of the problem for them."

"That's where I come in," Mallory said. "I will be quite literally flying under the radar. My broomstick will no longer be a mere Hallowe'en prop."

Lilith's eyes were wide with excitement. "Maybe I can help with the deliveries of the pills," she suggested. "That could save you some time – you would be freed up to go see the women who are having health emergencies."

Mallory smiled. "Yes – thank you!"

Lilith added, "I shall also set up an endowment to make your money grow. We don't want it to run out and have lots of women still needing help, looking to us for it, and us being unable to give it."

"Great!" Antoinette said. "This is why we need an attorney involved! Thank you, Lilith."

Lilith just smiled.

The doorbell rang.

Everyone jumped, and Specter got out of his bed.

Antoinette went to answer the door.

It was Jasvinder.

"How was your trip?!" Antoinette said, letting her in and hugging her both at once. She grabbed Jasvinder's bag as her guest toted her sitar in its case into the front hall.

Jasvinder sighed. "Long. And stressful. It used to feel like no big deal to enter your country, but now it makes me nervous. I tried not to show it, and they accepted my work permits. It took a little longer to get through with my sitar and everything because of the inspections, but I'm here."

"You're just in time to watch us set up our covert protest, to help women in forced birther states. That's what I wouldn't tell you over the phone."

They went into the living room, where Antoinette introduced Jasvinder to the assembled group.

Specter walked up to the newcomer and sniffed her sari, then rubbed up against her.

"Would you like a cup of hazelnut coffee?" Antoinette asked. "Or I could make you a cup of tea…I have a cardamom one."

"That would be very nice. Thank you," Jasvinder said. She was tired from traveling.

Antoinette's fiancé came home just then, greeted Jasvinder and the others, and carried the guest's things upstairs for her.

Jasvinder suddenly looked at Ileandra and did a double-take.

The alien smiled. "You know what I am, don't you?" she said.

Jasvinder was agape for a moment, but she recovered quickly. "Now that you have confirmed it,

I do. Wow…you're just sitting here among us, with a cup of coffee in your hands!"

Everyone laughed.

Ileandra said, "Yes…Earth's foods are fascinating. I'm a botanist, and that's what I'm here for: fruits, vegetables, and other edible things that I can take samples of to grow on my planet. Our ecosystem is depleted, and we need these things."

Jasvinder looked thoughtful, but said nothing.

She was too tired to think clearly, but had an idea. She would mention it later.

Antoinette brought her the tea and cut a piece of the torte for her. "Don't worry; we'll feed you something more substantial at dinnertime."

Jasvinder smiled and took a mouthful of the torte. After eating airplane food, it tasted wonderful. "So…tell me what you are up to. I can't stand the suspense any longer," she said.

Antoinette filled her in on the Silphium Society.

Jasvinder was amazed. "It is terrific that you are doing something like that! Congratulations! And don't worry; your secret is safe with me. Don't tell me the details, though. It is good that I know the general idea, but that's enough. I can follow along with the concerts and social calendar, and participate with the program without revealing anything more."

Antoinette smiled. "I knew you would say that."

The Janes

The dolls got to work, communicating with abortion pill suppliers, locating women who needed help, and putting a support system into place.

"We are the Janes," Antoinette said.

"What do you mean?" Willow asked, as she logged contact information and shipping data.

"The Janes were a secret group of women all over the United States who helped other women access abortion services when it was illegal, before *Roe v. Wade*," Lilith told her.

Willow's eyes widened as she took that in.

Lilith went on. "Some of them got caught, and as they sat handcuffed in a police van, they wriggled until they got the pieces of paper with patient names and other information out of their pockets, ripped them up, and swallowed them so that the women having abortions wouldn't be identified and arrested."

"Wow…" Willow was awed to hear that.

"It was the abortion version of the Underground Railroad run by abolitionists in the 19th century, when they helped slaves escape to Canada," Antoinette said. "And now Janes are needed again to do end-runs around the legal hellscape that American women have been forced back into."

Everyone looked at her, feeling determined and angry simultaneously.

"Perhaps we can induce the perpetrators to feel an impotent rage," Antoinette said. "After all, that's what drives misogyny anyway: both literal and metaphorical impotence on their part."

Grins all around.

"You do have a way of making us feel better," Nichelle remarked.

Antoinette smiled, and brought out bowls of chunky gazpacho for everyone.

It was delicious, and even Ileandra could manage to chew it with her small teeth.

This was followed up with zucchini bread, which was much appreciated by all, particularly Jasvinder, who was glad to have some light and homemade things to eat after 17 hours on a plane, with layovers, and then a taxi.

"That was just what I needed!" she said appreciatively.

"I'm so glad you liked it," Antoinette replied. "I knew you would; I always do after a long trip."

Jasvinder smiled as she ate her last crumb.

"I'll show you to your room so you can get settled," her hostess said.

With that, the meeting broke up. It was time for Jasvinder to rest before dinner.

The Silphium Society Commences

Jasvinder and Antoinette in Concert

Antoinette had told Jasvinder how beautiful the famous Elizabeth Park Rose Garden was. She had looked at some images of it online, but seeing it in person was quite a different thing.

It was spectacular!

They had arrived early so they could enjoy the garden for a little while, which was in full bloom.

The musicians would be performing together on a stage that faced it, separated by a huge, beautifully kept, verdant lawn for the concertgoers to sit on.

Ileandra was with them. She was wearing that same dress that Antoinette had brought out for her the day after her arrival because she liked it so much. "It even has strawberries in the pattern!" she said happily.

Antoinette laughed, pleased.

She and Jasvinder were more elaborately attired; Antoinette wore a gown with roses in various hues of pink and white, while Jasvinder had chosen a sari with a pink-and-white jasmine pattern on purple. Its ghagra matched the sari; her choli was a shade of pink that matched some of the jasmine flowers.

They glanced around as they got out of the car, which Antoinette's fiancé drove to the parking lot. Over at the stage, people were doing an activity called Yoga in the Park.

Jasvinder looked at them, happily doing asana and lotus poses in the fresh air.

"It's so cool here," she commented, "that doing all of this outside – yoga and a concert – is a comfortable experience."

"Oh, just wait another month. We have some intense heat waves in the summer thanks to climate change. And our Idiot-in-Chief is deregulating everything, gutting the Environmental Protection Agency, and letting polluting corporations go unchecked. There will be a lot of damage to repair when we finally get him out."

"Out, out, damned spot…" Jasvinder quoted.

"Indeed."

The dolls had walked over to the herb and iris garden and looked at the blossoms there. Antoinette still sounded angry, so her friend gestured to the sprawling rose garden across from it.

"Come and show me what you love about this place so much," Jasvinder pleaded.

Antoinette perked up and smiled.

The dolls went into the garden and looked at the roses, inhaling the perfume of many of them.

Ileandra went for the lighter-hued ones, which had the most intense scents.

The others listened to her explain this and followed her example.

They walked all around the beds of roses, the trellis paths, and up into the greens-covered gazebo, where they found people taking photographs on the seats and having a good time.

A little while later, Ileandra and Antoinette's fiancé sat down in lawn chairs facing the stage, and Antoinette and Jasvinder began to play.

It was classical fusion music: ragas for both violin and sitar. They had done this many times before, and were thrilled to be performing together again.

Soon a huge crowd of people filled the expanse of grass that stretched between the stage and the rose garden. Lawn chairs, blankets, wheelchairs, strollers – people had brought whatever they need to feel comfortable.

The other dolls arrived and found places to sit.

It was a lovely day, and soon the dolls were relaxed and happy, lost in the pleasure of playing music together.

Doll Pajama Party

The dolls were staying overnight at Antoinette's house in Connecticut. No one had to go home yet, so they had time to visit longer.

Antoinette was pleased when she found out that Willow's husband had had to travel for work, which meant that no one had to go home. Everyone had a pet cat except for Ileandra, but each cat had plenty of food and water for another night on its own.

"Let the pajama party begin!" Antoinette said.

Everyone was already wearing their pajamas.

"What is this, a Silphium Society pajama party?!" Lilith said. She was joking; she said it with a huge grin on her face. That was something to see, since she usually looked so serious.

"I guess so," Antoinette said, turning on the huge flatscreen TV in the living room. "What should we watch first?" It was the weekend, so there was no Bill Maher, Stephen Colbert, Jimmy Kimmel, or other routine show to watch. It was early in the evening, which meant that there was plenty of time for at least three movies.

They started with *Star Trek: First Contact*.

Tea was made, and soon everyone was settled onto the sofas, looking at each other's photographs on their iPhones.

Ileandra was fascinated to see images of the other dolls' cats, their families, and their homes. The witches' photographs were just as normal as the others' photographs; they were, after all, just people.

Meanwhile, they all enjoyed the movie, putting their phone down after about fifteen minutes or so.

Everyone laughed when Will Riker said to Geordi LaForge, "You told him about the statue?!"

"Poor Zephram Cochrane," Manon said.

The next movie was one that Antoinette had saved and recorded rather than from the On Demand menu. It was about Sarah Weddington and Norma McCorvey, the woman who became Jane Roe in the *Roe v. Wade* case.

Lilith had been very pleased when Antoinette said she had that. "I've always wanted to see that!"

So, they watched it.

"Isn't a case name supposed to say 'v.' rather than 'vs.'?" Mallory asked as the opening credits rolled. The movie was title *Roe vs. Wade*.

"It is," Lilith replied.

"I thought so," Mallory said, and said no more.

When it was over, Willow said, "That was terrible, that Norma McCorvey had to stay pregnant for the case. Otherwise, she could have found a Jane to help her get an abortion."

Lilith replied, "Now you understand what Machiavelli meant about government. He wasn't advocating that it should commit bad deeds, just observing how things work."

Nichelle said, "True. Now that we have watched a movie that is relevant to the purpose of our gathering here, can we have another frivolous movie next?"

Everyone laughed.

Antoinette picked up the TV remote control and looked through the choice.

"What is that one about?" Jasvinder asked.

She had pointed out the dystopian science fiction movie called *Don't Look Up*, in which the government gaslit the citizens as an asteroid massive enough to cause a Species Extinction Event approached the Earth. Denial of reality was how it dealt with the situation while those in power saved only themselves.

No one talked much during that one.

After that, everyone was tired enough to sleep.

The next morning, they all slept a bit late.

There was no urgency to leave for any reason.

It was a nice, leisurely weekend.

Antoinette brewed some toasted almond crème coffee from The Fresh Market and got out her waffle iron. It had a pretty heart pattern.

She made double batches of two kinds of waffles for everyone to enjoy: whole wheat cinnamon cardamom with raspberries, and walnut waffles with blackberries. There was plenty of maple syrup and orange juice to go with them.

The dolls loved it; everyone tried both kinds.

As they ate, the coffee took effect, making them fully alert for the day. Plans began to be discussed.

Mallory said, "I'm going to be using my broomstick a lot more now. I will have to travel at night, flying low to the ground. At least broomstick travel is faster than planes, trains, and automobiles."

Nichelle was looking at her oddly.

Mallory grinned. "I'm not kidding. Call me on the hotline that Willow is going to set up. I'll fly to Louisiana and help women in your state."

Nichelle still looked skeptical, but she smiled and said she would.

"I'm worried about the end of funding for PBS and NPR," Antoinette said.

"Well, it shouldn't be difficult to arrange some events for you to help with that," Willow said.

"Great! Let me know when and where."

Manon was listening with a wistful look. "I don't know how I can help with this effort, but I want to," she said. "So far, all I can think of to do is feed people's cats for them. Count me in for something else if you think of it."

"We will," Lilith said, "but you are in the process of applying for U.S. citizenship while having to travel for work between New York and Paris. Whatever it is, you will have to stay within those geographic limits."

"I know…but there must be something."

"We'll find it," Lilith said. "We just won't know what it is until we do."

Manon brightened up at this idea.

Jasvinder and Ileandra watched and listened.

"We're spectators in this," Jasvinder remarked.

"Yes," Ileandra said. "This is sad. That you need to fight this misogynist and fascist situation, I mean. Eons ago, my people went through all of this. And look where it got us."

She telepathically shared an image of her planet as seen from orbit.

It had smaller land masses than Earth, in different shapes. She indicated that they had once been much larger, but the warming of her planet had raised the sea levels.

The remaining land had some green, but just a little. It wasn't a lush, fertile planet.

It clearly showed why a botanist from that planet would visit Earth.

Everyone was quite startled.
And appalled.
"Sorry. But you get it even more now," the alien said, and everyone nodded.

The weekend wasn't over just yet.

Antoinette had planned another concert in Elizabeth Park the next day. It was a short one, though; she really just wanted to share some fun time with her friends and get to know the newcomers a bit more before they settled into work for the Silphium Society.

It is always better to get to know the people you are working with. She wanted to do as many activities as possible with the group before they all dispersed and went back to their routines.

The dolls wandered off in pairs, enjoying the roses and chatting.

It was great to spend more time with Jasvinder and hear about her fiancé, her sister, her life playing for movies in Bollywood, and whatever else her old friend felt like sharing with her.

Ileandra and Willow went through the herb garden. Willow watched as the alien botanist scrutinized each plant, and served as a lookout while Ileandra snipped samples and put them in her kit bag. The alien had prepared a container to preserve each leaf in stasis.

Willow caught glimpses of it, but knew that she wouldn't be able to describe it in enough detail for a scientist on Earth to replicate it.

The alien seemed totally unconcerned about that.

"You really grew up in a cold climate?" she asked. "I know about snow, but I haven't ever felt the cold much…just early autumn weather here."

Willow knew Ileandra's planet was overheated due to past use and abuse of its ecosystem.

She told the alien, "Yes. I grew up in Quebec City, far north, where it is covered with a thick layer of snow during the winter. We have so much snow and ice that in February, we have a festival of snow sculptures, with a mascot called Bonhomme. He looks like a clown made out of snow, with a red hat that hangs down on one side, with a tassel. He has huge black eyes, and a smile on his face."

"Does this keep your mind off of the cold?"

Willow laughed. "Well…it does for the duration of the festival. But I left, and went to Montreal for college, and then even farther south for graduate school. You can't escape the cold entirely here, though; the winters are still intensely cold, and our summers are hotter than they used to be. The difference seems to be a lot less snow, which messes with growing seasons."

The alien was listening to her intently.

"I know that having less snow means that water reserves don't get replenished. And glaciers that have existed on your planet for eons are melting."

"Yes, they are. I tend to forget that if I go home to my parents for Christmas. And we have wildfires that cover our province with smoke in the summer. That will likely start soon, so you'll experience it. It wafts to this area, so we will have to stay indoors when it gets here."

The alien had finished sampling the plants, so they wandered off toward the lathhouse and the sunken walkway beyond it. Lilith and Mallory were in there, by the dogwood trees.

The witches smiled when Willow and Ileandra caught up with them.

"We were admiring the twists of the yew trees. They are very flexible and beautiful. And…they make excellent broomsticks," Lilith said.

"So do oak trees," Mallory added.

Willow and Ileandra listened to them.

Willow was thrilled to hear them talk about this. It felt like being let in on a magical secret, which it probably was.

Ileandra considered this seriously, but without her usual interest, because those trees were not foods.

The witches sensed this and were amused.

Ileandra asked Mallory, "You are both a witch and a scientist. Don't you find it incongruous to deal with both magic and science?"

Mallory smiled and said, "Magic is just science that hasn't been explained yet."

"Oh…that helps. Thank you," the alien said, smiling back.

Manon and Nichelle were in the rose garden.

They couldn't get enough of the roses!

"We have lots of lovely roses in Paris and Belgium, but it is always such a treat to wander around slowly inhaling their scent," Manon said.

"We have them in New Orleans, too, and I feel the same way!" Nichelle replied.

It was a relaxing vacation from their usual lives.

Craft Fair

Nichelle had gone back to Louisiana. She needed to get back to her graduate students, she had told her hostess, but she had thoroughly enjoyed her visit.

Mallory had patients to see, so she left, happy and full of plans to actively resist the legal hellscape that so many women were enduring. "At last," she told Antoinette, "I can see a way to help them. Thank you for bringing me into this!"

Jasvinder needed to rest some more and practice for some upcoming concerts, and Ileandra wanted to stay with her, so the rest of the dolls left the house.

Antoinette had a gig at the local annual craft fair. Local artists would be performing in the parking lot behind the West Hartford Town Hall near the concessions section of the fair.

She wouldn't be on stage for long; the high school kids would be there for most of the afternoon, and it was mostly their show.

But she had been asked to participate, so she had agreed. The hope was that she could help draw a bigger crowd and thus help the fair to bring in more revenue.

She planned to wear a dress that she had bought at that fair some years past, with black and red raspberries on black. It was one of her favorites, and very comfortable.

She modeled it for her friends in her bedroom before they all went to the craft fair.

Lilith, Manon, and Willow admired the fabric and deep pockets, and said they hoped to find that vendor.

It was fun for them to wander among the stalls and see stained glass, handmade soap, beeswax products, photographs of birds and animals, wrought-iron garden sculptures, and jewelry.

Antoinette showed them one of her favorite vendors, an artist of a photographer who liked to travel around Europe with his camera in the spring and take images of lavender, roses, irises, and other flowers in gardens, on walls, and anywhere else that he found them.

They were impressed.

And then they found the dressmaker's stall, so of course they got dresses: Lilith found forget-me-nots,

Manon raspberries on white, and Willow found a cute bee-floral on butter yellow.

Later, upstairs at Antoinette's house, they tried them on, standing in a corner of an upstairs room together.

It was late in the afternoon by the time Antoinette was finished on stage. She put her violin into its case, regrouped with the others, and admired their new outfits.

Then they headed for the food trucks.

That was another fun part of the craft fair: fresh lemonade, smoothies of mango or strawberry-banana, and sandwiches with avocado, smoked turkey, lettuce, tomato, bacon, and pepper jack cheese on a brioche. There were sweet potato chips, and there was ice cream from local farms.

They sat at tables under tents in the huge town hall parking lot and laughed as the mayor of West

Hartford, a friendly and fun woman in her late fifties, did cartwheels in front of the stage and then sang along with the high school students.

"Wow," Manon said, "the mayor in my father's town doesn't do that. He just looks stern and tastes everything. At least he likes the pears that my father grows."

"Where is this?" Willow asked. "I thought you were from Paris."

"I am," Manon replied, "but my parents divide their time between Paris, where my mother is from, and Belgium, where my father's pear orchard is. That's in the Flemish Brabant, which surrounds the capital city of Brussels."

"So, you were raised in both places, then?" Lilith asked.

"Yes. It's been a fun upbringing, and I love going back to the orchard, even though I don't get much time anymore to do that."

"Speaking of time," Lilith said, changing the subject, "I have time to stay a little longer, and I have wanted to visit Ralph Nader's American Museum of Tort Law for a while."

Antoinette finished her ice cream and said, "Me too! Let's go tomorrow. We can take Ileandra and Jasvinder with us."

Invitation to Ileandra

Jasvinder listened to Ileandra talk about her work collecting foods from Earth to take home to her planet and cultivate there.

They were at Antoinette's house.

Jasvinder had stayed there to rest and practice her sitar music; she was tired from all of the excitement of traveling, arriving and immediately meeting several new people, and then giving a concert the next day.

Now that half of the visitors had left, she needed to practice before going on to the next concert, which would be at the Bushnell in Hartford.

She had booked a tour that would keep her in the Hartford area for two weeks, and take her to the Hartt School of Music, Trinity College, and the University of Connecticut at Storrs.

Antoinette would accompany her, sometimes to play, and sometimes just to keep her company and drive her.

The alien had stayed home to keep her company while the others went to the craft fair, and to type her notes for her memoir.

Antoinette had shown her the QWERTYUIOP typing system on the computer's keyboard. She had been amazed at how fast the alien picked it up. One round of "The quick brown fox jumps over the lazy dog" and Ileandra had been good to go.

Ileandra told her all about her mission. "Last time, I gathered whatever I could find growing outside, sneaking around to do it. Antoinette found me and gave me more things from her garden, and bought some other things."

Jasvinder listened with interest. "That must have been tricky to plan, not knowing when and how you could do everything."

Ileandra replied, "It was. When I went back, my colleagues were thrilled, and wanted me to visit again. They hadn't realized that we could work with humans. But Antoinette is very generous and determined to give me plants that I could only get with human help."

"That's terrific!" Jasvinder said, thinking.

"Yes, it certainly is. This time it's different; I can get things a little at a time and beam up to my ship for a few hours, get them settled, stable, and growing, and come back. I'm here for several months knowing that this is all part of a plan because I have a human friend to help me."

Jasvinder took out yoga mats as she listened.

"I love doing this," the alien said, and there was a tone of joy in her voice as she described each discovery: "Strawberries are still my favorite, but now that I've tasted figs and pistachios, I can't get enough of them. They are great additions to my collection."

"Would you like to visit me in India and go to the market to collect spices? Those taste wonderful, and combine to make many other tastes in different recipes. They come with lots of beneficial health effects, which my sister can explain to you. She practices Ayurvedic medicine. Oh, and mangoes! You need to get a mango tree to take home." Jasvinder was suddenly sounding as enthusiastic about food and the alien's work as Ileandra did.

The alien was listening to her with an expression akin to someone being told that it was Diwali and her birthday both at once.

"Yes! I would love to come and visit you!"

"Great," Jasvinder said. "How do we get you there, though…traveling around the Earth is complicated enough for a human, let alone an alien visitor to our planet…"

Ileandra chuckled. "Don't worry about that at all. Just go home on your own. I will return to my ship and have myself dropped off where you live in India."

"Oh! Wow…that's so easy. That's terrific!"

With that, they discussed the details of when and where to meet as they did various poses, including asana, the lotus position, and downward dog.

It felt good to stretch and move, and to know that a productive edible plant-gathering opportunity was in Ileandra's future.

India had seemed too daunting an ecosystem to the alien when she was sneaking around in the dark of night, collecting whatever she could forage.

This would be direct, and with a guide.

It was going to be terrific!

Mallory liked to be prepared.

To that end, she and Lilith were discussing current abortion law in the United States, specifically how late in a pregnancy a ban on it kicked in and in any other detail in each forced birther state.

As a physician, Mallory wanted to be aware of the legal ramifications of each action she took.

How should she dispose of expelled tissue so that it wouldn't be discovered and used against her patients later on?

"Burning is best," Lilith advised her. "The idea is to leave no evidence for prosecutors to work with.

We have to think of the actual tissue, plus any smoke that might possibly be seen during the burning."

Mallory looked at her. "But not every home has a fireplace..." she said, thinking it over.

"Well, flushing and burying have proved to be invitations for prosecution by the miscarriage police, so cremation is the way to go," Lilith advised her. "Look at states like South Carolina: 10 years in prison for not disposing of a miscarriage properly. Burn, tissue, burn, to eradicate any evidence!"

"Got it. I'll do it outside, away from any spot that offers a plain-sight view of what's going on."

Lilith paused, then said, "I'm trying to imagine this situation. How will you handle the interactions with your patients?"

Mallory considered this, then went into her kitchen to her stores of herbs. She came back to the sofa kitchen with little scraps of cloth, a roll of ribbon, and scissors, and put it on the coffee table.

"What is all this for?" Lilith asked, wanting to help with what was obviously a chore related to their discussion.

"I need to make a bunch of sachets to use on miscarried and aborted remains. It would be unseemly to simply set fire to them in front of the women, and perhaps their partners, without any sort of ceremony."

"You're right. It would make the women you help feel better about what is never a happy or pleasant experience. Simply burning to dispose of a problem as if no emotion were involved wouldn't do," Lilith agreed, picking up the roll of ribbon.

They sat there and made a hundred sachets.

From now on, Mallory's medical bag would contain sachets of fragrant herbs – lavender, rosemary, sage, and rose petals – for just such occasions.

"Irony of ironies," Lilith said. "During the Dark Ages in Europe, witches and other independent women were burned to death to take control of religion and health care delivery completely away from women, and now we're using fire to protect women from laws that prey on our independence."

Mallory looked up at her as she finished tying a sachet. "That also meant that the health care went from herbal potions that actually helped people to rubbish that did nothing for them, or poisoned them."

Lilith glared, thinking of that, and tied a bow.

All that mattered, ultimately, was that the women who needed abortion or miscarriage healthcare got it and that they got it without being bothered.

Which brought them to the other reason for the witches' visit that evening: Lilith was preparing a page for the Silphium Society's website on crisis pregnancy centers.

"I have plenty of law for it," she told her friend, "But I wanted to put the finishing touches on it during our visit, so that you could provide your input as a physician and gynecologist."

Mallory was delighted to help with this.

"That's terrific! The blackmail committed by those people is appalling. Help in exchange for agreeing to study the Christian Bible and learn its preaching by rote. Upon recitation of that, diapers are no longer withheld."

She looked at Lilith. "You probably already put that in, didn't you?"

"Well, yeah. That, and that they farm women's personal data so that they can track them throughout their unwanted pregnancies. But I was hoping you could comment about the fake doctors."

"Oh! Right…it's crucial that women learn to spot these fake sources of help and not even make contact with them. Real health clinics tend to be nearby, so these scammers set up shop to try to lure desperate women in…"

"Got that," Lilith said.

"The doctors are often not real ones. They're just liars claiming to be physicians, and they actually say that they provide abortions. But that's a lie, just to get women in the door," Mallory went on. "Once in, they will say anything to direct women to any other resources – such as temporary help until the pregnancy is carried to term…and then the women are on their own." Also, good luck researching these fake doctors to prove their credentials…"

She was looking at the web page. "I see you have cited a case, *First Choice Women's Resource Centers v. Matthew Platkin, Attorney General of New Jersey*, in which a crisis pregnancy center argues that it has a First Amendment right under freedom of speech to lie to women – to deceive, mislead, and endanger pregnant women. Good – they've given away their strategy and admitted their dishonesty in court."

"They also won't reveal who their donors are," Lilith said. "Unfortunately, we will have to wait for the U.S. Supreme Court's slip opinion to come out, and that could be at any time between hearing the case and the end of its term, which is next June."

"Slip opinion?" Mallory looked blank.

"That's what the court publishes its ruling in as soon as it is ready. Of course, now these things are also online, but before that, literal pamphlets that contained only one case's outcome were put out so that lawyers and journalists could see them immediately, not months later, when the next bound volume of *U.S. Reports*, the Supreme Court's publication, comes out," Lilith explained.

"Oh…" Mallory said.

"Anyway…I won't get into all that on this web page; I'll just explain that the ruling will come out later, after the justices write and release their opinions."

Mallory nodded. "With this court's makeup, I won't hold my breath for a ruling that requires truthfulness in assisting pregnant women."

Mallory was talking with Antoinette, who was visiting her in her New York City apartment.

Jasvinder had left the week before, and Antoinette was back in the city. She had a few concerts booked, and her fiancé was busy at the planetarium, gathering material for his students.

"Time is of the essence…and so is stealth."

She was talking about the logistics of helping patients who couldn't travel, couldn't get the physicians in their state to treat them when they needed abortion care, and were facing sepsis due to carrying a dead fetus.

"These doctors have been terrorized by the attorneys general in their states into believing that they will lose their licenses to practice if they give their patients abortion healthcare, even if that means letting a women die. That's not paranoia on their part, unfortunately."

"Just because you're paranoid, it doesn't mean that they're not out to get you," Antoinette said.

"Exactly. The problem is knowing who needs help. Your 'Contact Us' link with its promise of confidentiality and toll-free phone number is exactly what we need. I'm just waiting for a call."

Both of their phones buzzed.

It was a call from that hotline!

They looked at each other, excited to get the call, and then Mallory answered it. "Hello. This is Dr. Mallory Moonmist. How can I help you?"

She listened to the voice on the other end.

It was a woman in North Carolina who was in tears, her voice shaking. The woman described her situation. It was just the sort of case that Mallory had been concerned about: she was afraid that she might have to go septic before she could get help.

This woman lived near the Great Dismal Swamp, far from a hospital, and had been sent home to wait for her condition to worsen before the doctors would help her.

She didn't want to wait.

If she did, she could end up dead, or have her reproductive system destroyed from sepsis.

"Of course not! That won't be happening. Don't worry; I'll take care of you," Mallory assured her.

Mallory quizzed the patient over the phone, asking questions aimed at assessing her for toxic shock.

Bad news: it was starting already.

Good news: it was evening, and Mallory had gotten the GPS coordinates of the woman's house, which was in the woods, on a sparsely settled road.

"I'm coming to you now," Mallory told the woman. It will take me a few minutes to get there, so sit tight and wait for me, and we'll be meeting soon."

She ended the call and rushed to get ready to go.

Antoinette watched with delight as Mallory changed into an outfit that would enable her to blend into the area.

The Silphium Society was helping someone!

"I don't know how long I'll be," Mallory told her. "Will you take care of Maleficent for me?"

"Of course!" Antoinette said, petting the cat. Maleficent smiled at her. "Thanks!"
Antoinette and Maleficent watched as the gynecologist got her purple broomstick, went out to the fire escape, and mounted it.

Mallory took off into the darkening sky over Manhattan and headed south. She was gone in a flash, so fast that no one on the ground noticed.

It took Mallory roughly ten minutes to fly there. She moved fast, staying at a low enough altitude that her flight wouldn't interfere with airplane traffic, and keeping away from lights. The lights were a guide, but she didn't want to be illuminated by them.

Soon she was in the area of the Great Dismal Swamp National Wildlife Refuge. She could see it in the dimming light; it was a huge place with Lake Drummond in the center of it.

Off to the east was the street she was headed for. It had lots of houses on either side, but, helpful for the witch, there were patches of wooded areas behind the houses. She could land in the woods behind her patient's house and walk up to the back door from there.

She cast a spell to approach unnoticed, alit at the edge of the woods, and hid her broomstick, affixing it to a tree with a distinctive whorl that opened up into an owl's nest. The owl regarded her calmly as she did so.

Mallory took her phone out and called the woman back. "I'm here. I'm going to knock on your back door."

Her patient seemed anxious enough not to care to ask questions.

A light came on in the kitchen, and the door opened. A young woman with long, dishwater-blonde hair opened the door and peered out into the dim evening.

Mallory moved across the lawn fast, carrying her medical bag.

"Oh! There you are," the woman said. "Thank you so much for coming!"

"You're very welcome," Mallory said as they went in.

Her patient was having trouble moving; she was bent over, showing obvious signs of cramping, and she said that she was bleeding a little.

Spotting, it was called.

Her boyfriend/fiancé/husband – Mallory wasn't concerned to know what his status was – hovered around anxiously. He looked relieved to see Mallory.

"Let's go take a look," Mallory said.

"The sonogram said that the baby is dying," the woman told her, "But they won't take it out and let me recover. This is insane! I just want to be healthy enough to start over when I'm ready."

She was shown into the bedroom with the guy helping her patient get comfortable.

The witch made the smooth transition back to being a gynecologist and went straight to work, laying out her sterile tools. She directed the husband to boil water in their kettle.

"Do you have to pour hot water on me? Will it scald me?" the patient asked.

Mallory grinned. "No. That's just to keep him busy. My tools are all sterile, though I will wash them off before I leave."

"Oh!" the patient said, laughing in relief.

Mallory checked the woman carefully, confirmed that an abortion was necessary, and proceeded. The pregnancy wasn't far along, perhaps a bit more than three months – just enough for North Carolina's law to kick in and threaten this woman's health.

'Why couldn't lawmakers understand that the woman's health had to come first?!' Mallory thought to herself, not for the first time, as she worked.

She didn't even notice the husband hovering around, bringing towels and an empty baking pan for her to put the removed pregnancy into.

The fetus was tiny – roughly an inch and a quarter long – and dead. Its coloring wasn't that of a healthy fetus, either. It had died sometime before the patient had panicked to the point of calling the Silphium Society's hotline number.

Mallory gently placed it in the metal baking pan and returned her attention to her patient, quietly making sure that all placenta was out of her. It wouldn't do to have her get sepsis from the slightest bit left inside her after all this trouble.

All of it went into the baking pan.

What Mallory was doing was a dilation and curettage abortion, also known as a D&C.

Too bad she couldn't send the tissue for testing, just to find out the exact state of this woman's health.

That was a luxury, even though it shouldn't be one. Although…she did have a sterile plastic bag.

Then she told them, "It's going to be okay. No sepsis, though the fetus had already died when you called me. I'm leaving a course of antibiotics with you – pills to take. Take them until they are finished. You can try again if you want to in a few months."

She paused to let the couple look at the remains of this failed pregnancy.

"It's so small…" they said together, looking at it.

"Yes, it is. And I'm sorry, but we can't risk leaving it here with you. Do you have a fireplace?"

The husband looked at her, startled.

"We do. But no one burns anything in the summertime…and people might see the smoke."

"Let me help you with that."

They looked at each, then back at her, and nodded.

"They can't prosecute you for what they can't find," Mallory said, taking out her wand and moving the remains to the fireplace. She levitated every speck of the fetus and tissue into the fireplace, sprinkled some herbs over it all, and said a prayer:

"Triple goddess of the Moon, Earth, and children, we commit these remains to your care."

Flames shot out of her wand, incinerating it all.

A slight plume of smoke escaped from the chimney, but Mallory had put a spell on it, so it went unnoticed by the neighbors.

The couple stared at her.

She smiled. "I'm a real gynecologist," she told them. You can find me on the internet. And I'm also a witch, which is how I got to you so fast. But…who would believe you if you told them I'm a witch?"

"No one," they said, giving her the first smiles she had seen since her arrival.

"Thank you," Mallory said, smiling back.

With that, she picked up her bag and left.

Lilith Seizes an Opportunity

Lilith was about to take off on a trip.

She was fed up with what she had been doing: sitting safely at home, doing research and building a case file.

As a lawyer who loved having a nation of laws, Lilith was preparing for the restoration of democracy.

To do this, she had created a running case file, which she was building on daily, with each criminal act that Herr Pumpkingropenfuhrer committed, as well as those by his loyal minions.

The case file was a good thing to do, but she was itching for some action, and she had found it.

Her cat, Nostradamus, seemed to know that.

'He'll be fine: I'll ask Willow to come over and feed him,' Lilith thought to herself. 'If necessary, she will pack him in his carrier, collect his toys, and take him home with her until I get back.'

He had been watching her mutter to herself as she prepared to leave.

"Fascist regimes don't last forever. Eventually, democracy returns. History has shown us this repeatedly. Good and evil move in cycles. 'Just following orders' is no defense!"

Lilith was in quite an irate mood.

She was pleased with her efforts, and when the time came, this case file would be turned over to the International Criminal Court in The Hague, Netherlands – a court which was created by a treaty called the Rome Statute, thought of by a United States president, and an arm of the United Nations.

That same president had signed the Rome Statute on behalf of the United States shortly before his term ended, on the last day of the year 2000.

It was ironic that the United States was not a member of the ICC, but that was because the opposing political party – Herr Pumpkingropenfuhrer's party – objected to being subject to any court outside of its own country.

As a result, not only was the treaty never ratified by the United States, but the next president – from the opposing party – tried to unsign it.

There is no legal way to unsign a treaty.

And until the fascists were out of the Oval Office – the lot of them, not just the orange one – this was all just research. Lilith wanted something more substantial to do while she waited for that.

She kept reading and watching news reports as part of this documentation work, and one report in particular had caught her attention: there was a stockpile of contraceptives meant for women in developing and barely developed nations in sub-Saharan Africa.

This stockpile cost $40 million, and was made up of pills that were 10 years away from their expiration dates – perfectly good!

It was meant as U.S. AID gifts. But, like a maniac with a hatchet, the fascist in the White House had ordered the dismantling of U.S. AID, a program that was created by President John F. Kennedy for the purpose of soft diplomacy.

Soft diplomacy is the practice of helping those who need it so that they will be kindly disposed toward the nation that offers that help.

Not only had the orange fascist ordered the end of U.S. AID, but he had also ordered the destruction of this stockpile of contraceptives.

The stockpile was in a warehouse in Belgium.

Various organizations that worked to provide reproductive healthcare to women around the planet had offered to buy the contraceptives, repackage them, and ship them to their intended recipients, but no…the orange fascist and his team wanted them destroyed.

All they cared about was controlling women. They spouted some nonsense about birth control pills being abortifacients.

Women would thus be forced to endure pregnancies that they could not afford, to scrounge to feed the babies that resulted from those pregnancies, and many girls would end up dropping out of school due to unwanted pregnancies that their bodies were too young to carry.

Not as long as Lilith had anything to say about it!

She was going to that stockpile, and once there, she would send those birth control pills to hospitals near the women who needed them.

Antoinette and Manon were having dinner with their fiancés at Manon's place.

Lilith hated to bother them, but she was determined to go now, while she was excited about her plan…before she could talk herself out of it.

She called them and explained that she needed to go to Belgium under her own power, avoiding detection by customs and not have her passport checked. (She would bring it, of course, just in case.)

She did not say what she was going to do, but promised that they would soon know what she was up to.

They understood.

Manon said, "Don't worry. I'll ask my parents to take care of you. Just go ahead and do what you need to do."

"Thank you – thank you very, very much!" Lilith said, and rang off.

She glanced around, running over her plan in her mind one more time.

She might be back sooner than she thought, but just in case she wasn't, she called Willow and told her that she was going away, possibly for a few days. "Would you be able to come over and feed Nostradamus?"

Reliable as ever, Willow said, "Not to worry; I'll take care of him. Just call me when you get back."

Willow didn't ask any questions.

Good; Lilith located the warehouse using Google Maps. It was in Geel, Belgium. She prepared a list of GPS coordinates of every sub-Saharan hospital that the contraceptives were originally meant to be delivered to.

She laughed to herself, and realized that she was cackling in delight.

That just made her cackle some more.

This was going to be so much fun!

Just anticipating the outrage that would ensue later, when the deed was done and the pills were safely where they needed to be, was what put her in such a great mood.

Lilith wrote a note to her boyfriend, put her wand in her pocket, kissed and petted Nostradamus, picked up her broomstick, opened the window, stepped out, closed the window, and took off into the night.

Her cat watched her go with approval.

Lilith was excited as she flew across the Atlantic Ocean as fast as she could go. When had she last flown anywhere on her broomstick?!

She had to be covert about her activities as a witch, so she lived most of her life as other people did, moving about on foot and occasionally by plane, train, and automobile.

Not tonight!

It took her a couple of hours of flying, but Europe came into view as expected.

It was still nighttime.

Good.

She avoided major cities as much as possible, using the lights on the ground and sensing all of the people below her as a guide.

When she reached Belgium, she quickly found the warehouse and alit on its roof, considering how best to get inside and do what she needed to do.

Security guards patrolled the property.

That was no surprise.

She cast a spell to make them always walk away from her without realizing it. There; they would be unable to notice her.

Cameras…closed-circuit television…she cast another spell that made them unable to record her. If anything looked different, she wouldn't be in the images.

Time to go inside.

She flew down to the ground and alit by a door.

Pointing her wand at the keypad, she let herself inside and closed the door.

The place was quiet; few people were around.

And why would anyone worry?

They wouldn't be expecting a witch to visit.

She crept through the building and found the stockpile of contraceptives.

Boxes and boxes of them on pallets filled the huge concrete-floored room.

Time to get to work.

Lilith took out her phone.

It was bewitched to be impervious to technology that would betray her location and activities.

She opened the list of GPS coordinates.

Pointing her wand at the first set of boxes, she cast a spell. It was a one-way teleportation spell with the location of a hospital in Ghana.

Done.

Next: a hospital in The Gambia.

Next: another hospital, in Angola.

Next: one in Togo.

Benin. Mali. Côte d'Ivoire. Niger. Nigeria. Burkina Faso. Libya. Senegal. Guinea-Bissau.

Guinea. Sierra Leone. Liberia. Chad. Cameroon.
Sudan and South Sudan. Mauritania. The Central
African Republic. Eritrea. Djibouti. Somalia.
Damn, this was fun!

Lilith glanced around.
Her spells were holding. The guards were around,
but oblivious to her presence and activities.
Back to teleporting contraceptives:
Equatorial Guinea. Gabon. The Republic of
Congo. The Democratic Republic of Congo.
Uganda. Rwanda. Burundi. Namibia. Zambia.
Tanzania. (Stupid orange fascist – he pronounced
that one wrong on television!)
Malawi. Zimbabwe. Mozambique. Botswana.
Lilith looked up.
The boxes were all gone.

Wow…that felt…quick!

Time to go.

She had left her broomstick leaning on her shoulder as she worked. She took hold of it, putting her phone in her pocket.

Holding her wand, Lilith carefully made her way outside.

All was quiet until she was airborne again, and then…lights on, alarms blaring…and she was gone.

She was too tired to just fly home immediately, but Manon had made arrangements that solved that problem.

Lilith flew to a pear orchard in the Brabant just southeast of Brussels. She landed outside of the small cottage that Manon had shown her on her phone at the pajama party.

The door opened, and Manon's parents came out, ushered her inside, and gave her a fresh, perfect Anjou pear and some bottled water.

"Merci beaucoup," she said, and she meant it.

She was very tired suddenly.

Manon's mother smiled and brought her to a bedroom, where a nightgown was laid out.

She said "Bonne nuit," and left Lilith.

Lilith quickly changed, got into bed, and fell asleep.

The next day, Manon's father showed her around the orchard, making sure that no one else saw her.

She ate some delicious meals that day, starting with the most amazing waffles she had ever tasted and ending with moules et frîtes (mussels and fries), a classic Belgian meal. Pear cider was served.

When it was dark, she thanked Manon's parents profusely, exchanged hugs and kisses on each cheek with them, and flew off into the night, back across the ocean, and onto her fire escape.

Nostradamus was on her bed, smiling at her.

The next day, Lilith got up, ate breakfast with her boyfriend, kissed him good-bye as he went off to work for the day, and turned on the television.

MSNBC, CNN, and other stations were all talking about the same thing: the unexplained and seemingly inexplicable vanishing from a warehouse in Belgium of $40 million's worth of birth control supplies.

The journalists on MSNBC and CNN remained professional, doing their best to keep their facial expressions neutral, but their tone was a mixture of jubilation and mystification.

Lilith couldn't settle into her usual work routine.

She sat in front of the TV with Nostradamus, laughing to herself and being careful not to sip her coffee until there was a pause in the discussion. She didn't want to laugh involuntarily at a moment when her mouth was full of coffee.

But it was difficult, so she finished it quickly.

The woman on MSNBC seemed astonished as she said, "Footage from the warehouse closed-circuit cameras is puzzling, and it has been analyzed carefully for signs of tampering by hackers. The analysis came up empty every time."

'Of course it did,' Lilith thought, grinning.

"What it shows is a room full of boxes of birth control supplies that were soon to be shipped to France for destruction, and then, minute by minute, the boxes seem to – for lack of a better way to describe this – wink out of existence," the reporter continued.

Nostradamus purred and rolled up against Lilith. She petted him and listened some more.

"The White House released a statement in which the president was said to be furious with Belgian authorities. He accused them of stealing the supplies."

'Of course he did,' Lilith thought.

"The Belgian government has responded, saying that although it knows nothing about how the supplies vanished, if there are any other U.S. AID materials that the current U.S. administration plans to destroy, it would be happy to store them in that warehouse."

Lilith roared with laughter.

She got back to work for a while, but there were no new reports to save that were relevant to her ICC case file. Everything today was about that warehouse.

Around lunchtime, another MSNBC reporter came on with an update to the story.

"Reports are coming in from all over sub-Saharan Africa, where the birth control supplies were meant to go before the destruction order came. The reports say that hospitals have received their promised supplies, which appeared without explanation on their loading docks."

'That didn't take long,' Lilith thought.

The reporter continued, "This just deepens the mystery. But the staff at these hospitals are thrilled, and have sent messages of thanks to the White House."

Lilith shook with laughter.

"The White House is said to be outraged, and has sworn to investigate what it calls the theft of the supplies, and demanded their return."

'Oh really…!' Lilith thought.

"The African hospitals are not responding to that demand," the reporter said. "Instead, they are already busy distributing them to women who need them. I guess the 'no backsies' rule is at work here," she said, finally putting a reaction to the story into her delivery of it.

She looked pleased, but didn't let herself smile.

Lilith was enjoying this more than any movie.

She glanced at the clock. Early afternoon.

That meant that Antoinette was probably up and aware of all this by now.

Her phone rang.

Sure enough, it was Antoinette.

"Do those hospitals have you to thank?" she asked.

Lilith had put encryption charms on all of their phones, but Antoinette was still being a bit vague.

Lilith looked at her on the FaceTime feed. "Why would it necessarily be me?" she asked, with a coy smile.

"Because you are a lawyer, and this would require checking details such as exactly where to send everything. It doesn't require a doctor, so it doesn't have to be Mallory…and she's busy treating patients."

"Always the logical thinker – that's what you are. Nothing gets past you," Lilith said.

Antoinette grinned. "Did you see how angry Herr Pumpkingropenfuhrer is? And the outrage on Fox News? I tuned in just for a moment. I hate to give them any Nielsen ratings, but I just had to see…"

"Oh yeah. It's hilarious!" Lilith said.

"So, what brought this particular thing on?" Antoinette asked, curious.

"Watching the world go to hell wasn't enough for me. I have the power to do something, so I did it. I've been gathering data for a case file for the International Criminal Court, which means I just sit at my computer, compiling it all. I wanted some real action, so I took it."

"Well, that's the most awesome thing yet," Antoinette said, "and we're going to have more chances to do more wonderfully audacious things. Congratulations, thank you, and…I want to go on and on, but I'm sure you get the idea." She was grinning from ear to ear.

"Thank you, and I can't wait to do something else that both helps women and infuriates misogynists like this again soon," Lilith said.

They ended the call and got back to work.

Lilith left the news reports on.

They were just too much fun not to keep hearing as background sound for the rest of the day.

Nichelle had a boyfriend. He was another marine biologist, he lived in Louisiana, and yet…they had met in another state, far away from home, at an academic conference in New York. That figured…

Insert wry grin here, Nichelle liked to say whenever she explained how they met.

Her boyfriend specialized in otters. He loved them. Lots of North American river otters live along the banks of the Mississippi River delta, so he had plenty of them to occupy his time and attention.

Nichelle got a kick out of surprising him with a long, loose shirt that she wore on the beach. It depicted otters, and was cute.

Guys didn't usually pay that much attention to clothing patterns, but this one caught his eye.

He looked at the pattern all over, and was pleased to see that the otters on it were floating on their backs and in pairs.

The only detail missing was linked arms, which kept the pattern flexible for sea and river otters. Sea otters sleep with their arms linked so that they won't float away from each other, and will wake up together. River otters sleep on land.

Nichelle accompanied him as he visited each spot that the otters he studied were usually at. He observed the semiaquatic carnivorous mammals as they fished, swam, and played, rolling around in a spiral movement and scratching themselves.

The otters hunted for fish, eels, frogs, and other things, such as molting ducks, which were easier to catch. They also foraged for fruits, aquatic plants, and mollusks.

Halfway through the day, the couple left what they were doing to get lunch at a riverside restaurant. The place offered a vegetarian dish of Poblano peppers stuffed with cheese, tomatoes, onions, and with black bean rice, which they enjoyed.

While they ate, Nichelle asked her boyfriend how his research was funded.

The answer was that the Gordon and Betty Moore Foundation provided the funding. "They are based in San Francisco, and favor that area, but they fund projects all over the world, too."

"Good to know," Nichelle said, with interest.

Then it was back to work, if you could call it that when work was so fascinating and so much fun. The project was about the impact of climate change on otters and their habitat.

Nichelle was relaxing, though; she was just watching her boyfriend's activities and helping him collect and file data while enjoying the beautiful day.

Eventually, it was time to leave, so they headed back to New Orleans, pausing at her boyfriend's university – the University of Louisiana, located on the south bank of the river, to drop off the equipment and save the data to his office computer.

They made a brief stop at Nichelle's apartment before going out to dinner so that she could change her outfit and introduce her boyfriend to Nemo, her cat. Nemo loved boxes, so she kept a few here and there in each room.

Nemo was a big hit. He jumped in and out of his boxes, playing with Nichelle's boyfriend while she changed her clothes.

When she came out of the bathroom, ready to go, she was clean, comfortable, and pleased with the once-over look she got. She did look good.

She was also glad to see the cat getting along so well with him; Nemo had immediately taken a liking to this guy! Always a good sign…

Dinner was at Dakar NOLA. They ended their day with a spicy West African seafood meal, followed by a beautiful dessert – one each; they shared.

After that, it was time to go home. Nichelle had a big day coming up, because soon it would be time to launch the *Yemoja* for the summer.

She had a lot of preparations to make.

The Walt Disney Concert Hall

While Ileandra was away in India, Antoinette was away, too. She had a concert booked in the Los Angeles, in the hall designed by Frank Gehry.

Antoinette had been settling back into her routine of giving concerts and the travel that came with that. Meanwhile, she kept thinking about the fact that she was merely financing the covert efforts of the Silphium Society, but not involved with the action.

She couldn't do much about that, though. She would just have to be the public face that she as, keeping people's focus on her violin career. If anyone looked up the people involved, they would see that she was one of them. That would have to be enough.

Willow came along with her. Ostensibly, she was
there solely to help Antoinette with trip logistics, but
in reality, she had come to set up a branch office of
the Silphium Society in L.A. They stayed at the
Millennium Biltmore Hotel.

Antoinette played a montage of Disney movie
themes: *Cinderella, Sleeping Beauty, Bambi, Dumbo,
Mulan,* and *Moana.*

It was just a fun trip, really – routine, and it
reminded Antoinette of earlier, calmer times. It feels
like a nice escape from the insanity that the Silphium
Society was working against.

It was also nice to be away with her fiancé,
Antoinette thought, and Willow's husband had
gotten time off to accompany her. It was more like a
nice four-day weekend trip than anything else, and

everyone had a happy, relaxed time enjoying various restaurants and a change of scene.

They enjoyed the travel arrangements that Willow had made, staying at the Omni Los Angeles hotel. It was important for the sake of the quality of the concert to arrive a day ahead, so they did, hence the lovely long weekend.

That hotel has a restaurant that offers French cuisine, called the Noé Restaurant & Bar. Its menu offered a fall pear salad with ingredients that Antoinette loves: mixed greens, blackberries, goat cheese crumbles, candied walnuts, topped with a balsamic tarragon vinaigrette. She thoroughly enjoyed it.

Willow tried the prawn croquette, which was made with prawn croquette a lemongrass tomato reduction, yuzu aioli, and chives. She was curious to taste them because croquettes are part of Québécois cuisine.

The guys tried the same things for starter plates. For dinner, however, they each wanted the Thai coconut chicken with vegetable rice noodle salad, crushed cashews, and Thai chili sauce.

The women each had a taste. They liked it, but they enjoyed what they had ordered even more: the seared Quinault wild salmon (named for a Pacific Northwest tribe). It seemed to have been given a southwestern twist, with Poblano pepper, green onion, tarragon, Masago roe, roasted tomato, and drizzled with a sake corn reduction. It was delicious, and they weren't at all sorry to have ordered it.

The guys both said that they wished they had gotten the salmon. Oh well!

For dessert, the group decided to order one of everything and share it. It was fun; they had coconut butter cake, Mexican chocolate mousse, and banana pudding crème brûlée.

"This is all part of the fun," Antoinette said, when the guys wondered why she knew so well just what to order. "Great food is crucial when traveling. It makes up a huge portion of the trip. If that isn't planned carefully, it can ruin a trip."

"Oh…" Willow's husband said. He got it then. He was a sound engineer for television productions in Manhattan; food wasn't his thing, but he did enjoy it…particularly the coconut butter cake.

Willow grinned as he scraped his plate with his fork savoring every last bite.

The day of the concert, Saturday, Antoinette spent at the concert hall in rehearsal with the orchestra. She ate at the café in the building, and enjoyed a fancy latte with a leaf pattern in the foam. By evening, she was ready for perform with that group of musicians, with whom she had played several times before.

Willow, meanwhile, visited the premises of the Silphium Society branch office, met with a gynecologist classmate (from medical school, not witch school!) of Mallory's, and set it all up, complete with a connection to the hotline.

This physician couldn't travel like Mallory could to another state in under an hour on a broomstick, but she was committed to the cause of delivering reproductive and abortion healthcare to women in forced birther states.

She knew all of the stealth methods of delivery of care, particularly not putting her own name on anything, and not releasing healthcare records to attorneys general or other controlling, misogynist enforcers.

Willow's husband decided to go to the Griffith Observatory with Antoinette's fiancé. They met with the astronomers there, including a colleague and graduate school classmate of his.

Everyone had a fun and productive day.

They met at the concert hall in the evening, and attended Antoinette's performance. Her fiancé came prepared, with a beautiful bouquet of pink roses for her – her favorite.

The rest of the weekend was spent visiting art museums and enjoying other restaurants. The area has plenty to offer. Sunday, they visited the J. Paul Getty Museum and Getty Villa, which the group could tour in one stop; Monday afternoon they went to the California Science Center before boarding their plane back to New York City.

Antoinette's fiancé said he could get used to traveling with her.

She grinned, pleased to hear that.

Manon had an interesting auction lot coming up: rare books from the 18th century. The books for sale were particularly notable for their condition, which is excellent, plus their completeness, provenance, and the fact that all are limited editions.

The auction would include an opportunity for the potential buyers to view the items up close before the bidding commenced. People would be walking around, looking closely at each item under a curator's supervision.

The curators had been asked to dress imaginatively, in something relevant to the events.

Manon needed to find a suitable outfit to wear, and she didn't have time to get something that specific made.

When she mentioned this to Mallory, she was suddenly in luck.

"I am a purple witch," her friend said. "I love all things purple, so most of my clothes show at least some of that color. I have a dress that I got for that reason more than any other, but it happens to depict the endsheets of old books, and you can wear it if you like it."

Endsheets are the strong and often decorative papers that are attached to the hard cover of a book on one half and to the interior of it on the other half. These sheets could have solid colors, or depict a botanical theme, of swirls of color. Designs on them include cloud marbling and fan marbling.

Manon visited Mallory and tried the gown on. It was modeled after 18th century ball gowns, but with deep pockets, and the bodice and polonaise depicted an historically accurate fan marble pattern – perfect!

"Thank you very much, Mallory! I really appreciate it. This will be so much fun to wear."

"You're welcome!"

The event wasn't until the end of the week, so with that business taken care of, the dolls moved on to talking about the Silphium Society.

Mallory told Manon that she had a nice stockpile of abortion pills ready to use, plus, as always, a medical kit packed so that she could leave with it at a moment's notice.

"That's just part of being a doctor," she added, "but now I have this in the kit."

She brought out a plate of lavender butter cookies, made cups of blueberry-lavender tea, and the two of them sat down to enjoy it.

"Do you ever worry about getting caught?" Mamon asked, worried about her.

"Not exactly, no," Mallory replied. "I'm careful, of course, flying under the radar – literally – and casting spells that help. And I won't put my name on any prescriptions that could induce some hostile state's attorney general to sue me and try to extradite me to that place, or levy some financially debilitating fine on me."

"So much to be careful of," Manon said.

"Indeed," Mallory replied.

Botanical Shopping Spree

It was a beautiful sunny day in Manhattan. Antoinette and Manon both had the day off.

Ileandra was with them, and they were going to take her food shopping. Both Antoinette and Manon were gourmet cooks and bakers, so they knew where to go for the best of everything.

The alien was excited, to say the least.

"Where will we go?" she asked.

Antoinette said, "The farmer's market in Union Square, to start with. It's open from 8 a.m. to 6 p.m. today, so we'll start there before they run out of the best and most interesting things. I'm hoping for squash blossoms and goat cheese. Chèvre, to Manon," she said, grinning at her friend.

"Oh…dinner tonight is going to be a treat," Manon said, happily anticipating not only plying Ileandra with gifts for her planet's gardens, but also an evening of cooking. "Our fiancés will be eating with us, so that's dinner and dessert for five."

"We're also going to take you on an online shopping spree for many varieties of many fruit trees so you can take them home and grow them on your planet. We'll do that when we get back."

Antoinette was full of plans.

Ileandra was getting more excited by the minute.

She just had one question.

"How will we store it all until we get to Connecticut, so I can have it all beamed up to my ship? And when will we be back there?"

"Tomorrow. I planned this so that you wouldn't have to worry about keeping the items long. We're all driving back there tomorrow, so you can have it beamed up tomorrow night. Don't worry; I know that your boyfriend will be taking care of it in short order," Antoinette added with a grin.

Ileandra grinned back, and then said, "I will have to stay on the ship for a couple of hours to settle everything into place."

"No problem – we won't be leaving Connecticut right away. You'll have plenty of time do everything you need to do. Besides, the plants won't arrive until much later. I'm glad you're here for a nice, long visit, and not just because I'm happy to have you here. This will give the plants time to arrive."

"Logistics can take a while to play out," Manon commented.

Ileandra nodded.

Everyone finished their coffee, petted Specter, and they left Antoinette's apartment.

Ileandra noticed that Antoinette and Manon were each armed with food shopping bags. They carried bags that contained several folded-up bags.

'Wow,' she thought, 'how wonderful it must be to have a planet that produces that much fabulous food available for the taking…'

The farmer's market was called the Greenmarket. It consisted of a collection of white canopied stalls all over Union Square.

Antoinette and Manon kept the alien close by, but seemed happily distracted by the abundance of everything fresh, artisanal, and beautifully colored around them.

They found the squash blossoms first, which was good because they were selling out fast. Next came the goat cheese – chèvre, Manon insisted on saying again. It came in various forms: plain; cranberry; and chive. They bought all three kinds.

They also bought fresh figs and honey.

"This is where we buy things that we won't see elsewhere," Manon said. "We have to carry it all, so we need to plan carefully."

Ileandra nodded. She took a bag of fresh flowers to carry that included a profusion of pinks, whites, and reds. Their scent was sweet, and like nothing she had encountered before. "What did you buy?" she asked them.

"Sweet William – bouquets with every color it comes in," they told her. Antoinette was going to bring hers to Connecticut. She had bought one for her mother, too. Manon would take hers home.

Chelsea Market was next. That place was amazing; it had a store called the Manhattan Fruit Exchange. "Actually, they changed it to the Manhattan Fruit Market and gave it a makeover," Antoinette said. "It was fine the way it was, but marketers can never leave things alone."

Ileandra looked like a kid in Willy Wonka's chocolate factory as she stared open-mouthed at everything.

Manon laughed, but admonished her to keep her facial expression neutral so that she wouldn't attract unwanted attention.

The alien started, then closed her mouth. She did want to focus on the food and nothing else today!

The place had aisle after section after shelf after display of herbs, mushrooms, cheeses, fresh and dried fruits, nuts, vegetables, and herbs. It was beautiful.

"You should see it at Hallowe'en," Antoinette said. "Artists carve pumpkins with a huge variety of facial expressions, trees with branches, cats, you name it. They have special tools and amazing talents."

Ileandra nodded, speechless and delighted.

Her friends bought pistachios, mascarpone cheese, sweet potatoes, asparagus, and a few different kinds of mushrooms.

They paid and left the store.

"Where else will we be going?" Ileandra asked.

"There is a terrific fish store here. If the smell bothers you, there are lots of interesting stores to look at in the hall, and some benches. But if not…"

The alien was curious, so she went with them.

The Lobster Place sold much more than lobster. Shellfish of all sorts, finfish, all on displays of ice was spread out before them.

Manon went straight over to the mussels and bought three pounds of them.

Antoinette bought four fillets of Arctic char.

That was it; they didn't linger because it didn't seem right to keep the alien in there for longer than necessary.

And they had more plans for the day.

But they did walk all around Chelsea Market with her and show her everything there was to see: bakeries that specialized in bread, bakeries that specialized in brownies and other desserts, a cheese store, a book store, and so on and on.

After their walk was over, Antoinette and Manon were hungry. They weren't having trouble carrying all that they had bought, but they wanted to stop and eat, so they took Ileandra into a farm-to-table restaurant that they had paused at earlier.

The menu looked tempting. It was like eating at a restaurant catered by the Greenmarket. Everything was fresh and perfect.

They each had a salad, but those salads were way above average in terms of content, presentation, and inventiveness. Each one was different – they wanted to try a few options from the menu, after all – and it filled them up.

Apricots, scallions, chives, pepper jack cheese, nasturtiums, pine nuts, pecans, almonds…fresh balsamic vinegar, champagne vinegar, raspberry vinegar, extra-virgin olive oil…what a treat!

"Why do they call it 'extra-virgin'?" Ileandra wanted to know.

"Because it's pressed three times," Manon said. "That gives it the best flavor. We use it to cook lots of recipes."

"Oh. It's delicious."

The other dolls nodded, smiled, and kept eating.

Dessert was ice cream. But it wasn't the kind of ice cream that the alien had experienced before. This was gelato. It was Italian, soft, smooth, and had a texture that she couldn't quite figure out.

"It's aerated and has less fat than other ice cream," Antoinette told her.

"Oh…interesting…and so good!" Ileandra said, spooning another mouthful of dulce de leche.

Manon had hazelnut; Antoinette had pistachio.

When they were finished eating it, they went back to Antoinette's place, put the food away, petted and fed the cat, and sat down in front of Antoinette's computer.

"Let the alien shopping spree begin!" Antoinette said, opening up tabs for websites that included White Flower Farm, Hale Groves, Burpee, and the Arbor Day Foundation.

"We're going to buy you lots of fruit trees," Antoinette said.

"We're splitting the cost," Manon added. "And…my father will be giving you one each of his pear trees, so that will be another stop for you to make, in the Brabant region of Belgium, to beam them up. He has Anjou pears, mostly, but some other varieties."

Ileandra's mouth dropped open. She shut it, and then said, "Thank you both very, very much!"

They had lots of fun choosing red, black, and golden raspberry bushes; golden, red, and black cherry trees; blueberry bushes; plum trees; peach trees (fourteen different trees!); apricot trees; black, purple, and Olympian figs; grape vines with black, red, green, and champagne varieties; and many apple trees, which included Red Delicious, Golden Delicious, Pink Lady, Fuji, Honeycrisp, Honeygold, and McIntosh.

"Some companies have things that others don't," Antoinette said, which meant that they bought blackberry plants, strawberry plants, currant plants, and vines for honeydew and cantaloupe melons from Burpee's, figs from both White Flower Farm and the Arbor Day Foundation, and raspberry plants from all three.

Strawberries got some special attention; Antoinette knew it was Ileandra's favorite fruit, so she bought every kind she could find. It thrilled her to see the alien looking so happy.

Antoinette insisted on buying two kinds of orange trees from Hale Groves.

Ileandra was thrilled; drinking fresh squeezed orange juice was something that she had come to love about visiting Earth.

Next came the vegetables.

That meant loading up the virtual shopping cart with a virtual feast.

Heirloom tomatoes: black Krim, yellow, red, etc.

Squash, beans, a rainbow of carrots, hot peppers, red, orange, yellow, and purple bell peppers, arugula, broccoli, beets, corn, kale, cucumbers, garlic, peas, potatoes, onions, pumpkins, radishes, leeks, lettuce, spinach, and watermelons.

"Don't eat the seeds," Antoinette warned. "They're full of cyanide; take them out."

Ileandra nodded. Actually, she knew that, but now she was actually planning to work with and eat watermelon. She had avoided it for just this reason, but her people were careful; they would bother to remove the seeds before eating the fruit.

Then came the herbs: basil, lavender, chervil, chives, and dill, plus parsley, sage, rosemary, and thyme (that group of four led to Antoinette singing the Simon & Garfunkel sone for the alien).

That concluded the online gardening shopping spree. Antoinette and Manon closed it out with their credit cards, and turned their attention to the evening meal.

Antoinette prepared the squash blossoms by carefully stuffing them with goat cheese, added sliced strawberries to the plates, and drizzling it all with a little balsamic vinegar.

Manon cleaned the mussels in cold water, de-bearded them, and steamed them over a broth of saffron, white wine, butter, fresh chives, and salt and freshly ground black pepper.

She made fries out of the sweet potatoes, which was an elaborate process to watch, but well worth it. The potatoes were cut into julienne shapes, then fried, then put in cold water, then fried again. Finally, they were put in wax pepper and sprinkled with salt.

Antoinette cooked the mushrooms in butter with salt and pepper, stirring often, and the asparagus in a mixture of extra-virgin olive oil, butter, fresh dill, and salt and pepper.

She seared the Arctic char in butter with sherry wine and a little salt, then poured the liquid over the fish when she plated it.

For dessert, Antoinette made a sweet buttery tart crust, which she filled with mascarpone cheese. Sliced figs went over it with pistachio nuts, which she drizzled with honey.

The fiancés felt spoiled as they ate their way through it all.

Bon appétit!

Alumnae in Salem, Massachusetts

The school where the witches had met was having a reunion for their class, so they decided to attend it. It would be nice to see their classmates.

Lilith had dropped her cat off at Antoinette's place, and Mallory had left Maleficent with Manon and Dauphine. The cats got along, so it would be fine; satisfaction to all.

The witches dressed for the occasion and took off into the night, happy to be out flying together.

Soon they were in Salem, Massachusetts.

"It looks the same," Mallory said, looking at the lights from above.

Lilith laughed. "Of course it does. It won't get overpopulated with all of the spells on it."

They alit in the garden of the Ropes Mansion.

It was early evening, just after dark, and quiet, just the way they needed it.

They got off of their broomsticks, put them up inside a tree on the perimeter, and bewitched them to blend in until the next evening, when they would be ready to go home. Even if it rained, the broomsticks would stay dry and unnoticed.

They came out of the garden, turned onto the sidewalk, and started walking.

"Here we are in Salem, Massachusetts," Lilith remarked, "dressed in full witch regalia. This is one of the few places on the planet where dressing as what we are will attract no notice whatsoever."

Mallory laughed. "True," she replied.

They were between Federal Street and Essex Street, with lots of historic houses all around them, plus some museums on the corner of North Street and Essex.

Their school was in this area.

But the events were for the next day, so they walked out onto the sidewalk of Essex Street, turned right, which took them southwest, and walked to the Salem Inn, where they had booked rooms.

Actually, they had planned to each get their own room, but changed their minds when they found out that it had one haunted room and they both wanted to stay in it.

The concierge had laughed when they had arranged this over the phone and said that it was good that they were two old friends staying there together in case it got scary for them. And then she had booked the room for them to share.

The room was in West House (the inn had three houses, the others being Curwen House, which didn't take children, and Peabody House). It was West #17 – all theirs for one night.

"It's nice," Lilith said as they walked in and plopped their bags in a corner, looking around.

Mallory went into the bathroom to freshen up and said, "There's a nice walk-in shower. It's all done in white marble."

A flatscreen TV was mounted in the corner, titled down from the ceiling to face the bed.

Lilith was really hoping to see or hear a ghost.

"There's a woman named Katherine, a boy who runs up and down the stairs, and a cat – three ghosts."

Mallory laughed. "You don't actually expect them to forego the fun of startling you, do you? You'll have to relax and fall asleep before you sense anything."

Lilith didn't care. "It's part of the experience."

They left to eat dinner, which they had planned to eat at a nearby restaurant. Well, nearby to New Yorkers who were used to walking.

The concierge, a nice woman who was their age, was surprised that they intended to walk to the Sea Level Oyster Bar, which was east of the inn, on Wharf Street.

"We're used to walking; it's no big deal," Lilith assured her.

Mallory nodded, and off they went.

It was a brisk walk, but they arrived in time for their reservation and got a table with a view of the wharf and Salem Harbor.

After perusing the menu, they decided to have salads – beet and field greens for Mallory; and a spicy citrus salad for Lilith – and fried oyster tacos for the main course. The tacos came with citrus jalapeño slaw, pepperjack cheese, and roasted red pepper tartar sauce. It was all very good.

They split an Almond Joy chocolate torte for dessert. Perfect!

After a brisk walk back to the inn, the witches got ready for bed, turned on the TV to watch *The Late Show with Stephen Colbert*, and then tried to sleep.

Lilith was a bit excited and had trouble dozing off until Mallory told her that she would never see or hear the ghosts until she relaxed. "Try counting broomsticks or something. I'm going to sleep."

Lilith did that, and soon nodded off.

In the middle of the night, they woke up to the sound of rapid, small footsteps in the hall. They opened their eyes and a woman was walking across the room. Katherine was wearing a long dress. And a specter of a cat was sitting up on the windowsill, facing them.

But, as soon as they sat up for a closer look, it all stopped and vanished. Damn!

Mallory laughed. "Typical of ghosts."

Lilith looked at her, then grinned. "At least we saw and heard it all! That was great."

At breakfast, they had omelets and fresh fruit with coffee, and asked the couple who owned the inn about the ghosts.

"You saw and heard them, then?" they said, smiling.

"Yes, we did," they said, smiling back.

"And you weren't scared at all?"

"No. They seemed nice."

The innkeepers told them a bit of background on the ghosts.

The witches thanked them and left, happily full of good food and company.

They had some time to kill before the reunion, so they visited Proctor's Ledge at Gallows Hill on Pope Street, where the Salem Witch Trials victims had been hung.

This was something they always did when they were in Salem, to remember how viciously humans can treat anyone who is a bit different from the majority.

Of course, rotting rye flour full of mold that contained PCP, a strong hallucinogen, didn't help much with that, either.

The victims of the trials were not given marked graves. They were simply buried like criminals. Their families may have reclaimed them in secret after the fact, but no one knew where they were buried.

Proctor's Ledge is just a semicircle on the side of the road made of stone with the victims' names in the wall, and benches to sit on, with the year "1692" carved in black at the entrance to the tiny, open spot.

After that, Lilith and Mallory walked to the Salem Athenaeum to look at its collections of rare books. This was where they had spent lots of time during their years in school together, doing their homework and researching term papers.

It was a beautiful library, and the staff remembered them, so the visit to it brought back pleasant memories.

At the reunion, everyone was talking about politics and wanting to help people.

"I've never found so many reasons to use magic before," Mallory told Lilith once they were seated. "And, apparently, we have plenty of company in that."

Lilith gave her a wry grin. "Of course you haven't. It's always when the world is manifesting more evil and ill intent that we end up using it more."

Theirs had been a small class of just twelve people, so it was an intimate affair in which conversation with everyone present was possible. Lilith's dress was admired by all for its kaleidoscope of black cat faces.

It was an enjoyable evening. They sat with their old classmates and teachers, shared news of their lives – and cats! – and ate a good meal.

It ended with the perfect dessert: devil's food cake with a devil's trident made of red decorator's sugar shaken over the chocolate frosting.

The cake was as scrumptious as it looked, too.

When the event was over, Mallory and Lilith said good-bye to their old friends and walked out into the darkness, to the tree in the garden of the Ropes Mansion to retrieve their broomsticks.

Soon they were airborne, on their way home.

Lilith was furious…again.
She was visiting Antoinette, and all fired up over the latest attack on women's bodily autonomy.

"Indiana has announced new enforcement measures to control women's bodies and punish anyone who has an abortion."
"What are they?" Antoinette wanted to know.

The Indiana Department of Health, or IDOH, is going to keep a computer database called DRIVE, for Database Registration of Indiana's Vital Events. It will track every birth, death, and abortion. Hospitals that refuse to hand over this data will be fined and face disciplinary action. Every abortion report will be scrutinized by law enforcement to determine whether or not the abortion was 'merited,' whatever that means to them."

Mallory was there, too. She looked horrified.

"I can't fix every facet of this problem…" Lilith said, trailing off, thinking.

"We know you can't," Antoinette said.

"We don't expect you to deal with that aspect of it, either," Lilith assured her. "I'm going to take care of it with a little hacktivism. That database and any backup of it is never, ever going to work. All abortion files will be continuously corrupted once IDOH gets them. Every single time."

She grinned mirthlessly as she said this.

She didn't need to say more.

The others simply returned her grins, delighted with her efforts.

Graduate Student Aid

"Professor, I'm so sorry to bother you with this," Jeanne said, sounding close to tears.

Nichelle had gone to visit her, expecting to discuss the details of her grant funding, which had just come through.

She had wondered why Jeanne had seemed so anxious for the entire time that they were out eating dinner in San Antonio.

Now she knew.

Jeanne's 12-year-old niece, Callie, needed – and wanted – an abortion.

Jeanne was determined to make it happen.

"Something bad happened at a sleepover party," Jeanne said, starting to cry. "From what I was able to find out, her friend's older brother was watching the kids, and he put a date-rape drug in her punch. I can't believe it! She looks mature for her age, but he knows she's twelve, the evil rapist!"

Nichelle let her rant, just listening.

"Now that Texas has legalized spying on other people and tattling on them for money, we don't know how to help her in time. We don't have money for traveling to other states. I hate it here. I'm going to finish my Ph.D. and find work in a pro-choice state. Maybe Hawaii. I wish I were done already. I'd take her with me and get her out of here."

Nichelle nodded and smiled. She said, in a distinctly wry tone, "So…Texas is in for some serious brain drain when you leave. They've certainly been begging for it with a governor and attorney general who are so set on controlling women…and young girls."

They were in Jeanne's parents' home. The house was small, but she had had her own space all through college, even when her grandmother came to live with them.

But now her niece was there, thanks to a flood that had washed away her home along with her parents, so Jeanne was sharing her room with her.

"We can't call the police without revealing that Callie is pregnant, because then we won't be able to even think of traveling out of state for an abortion…and she's too young to stay that way!" Jeanne raged, starting to cry again.

"Damn this legal hellscape. That boy should be behind bars," Nichelle said.

With that, Nichelle took out her phone, called the Silphium Society hotline, and hoped that she would get lucky and Mallory would answer.

'What if Mallory wasn't available?' she worried to herself. Mallory could be with a patient, or doing surgery at her hospital, or who knew what else.

But no…Mallory answered on the second ring.

Nichelle greeted her.

"Hey, Nichelle! It's good to hear your voice, but I suspect it's not good to hear it on this number. What's going on?" Mallory asked, coming right to the point.

Nichelle filled her in, and gave her their location.

"Okay. Please stay where you are, and I'll see you in a couple of hours."

"A couple of hours?" Nichelle echoed, amazed.

"Yes. It'll take me that long to fly there."

"You can just hop on a plane and find a flight that gets here that fast?!" Nichelle couldn't believe it.

Laughter on the other end.

Mallory sobered up quickly and replied, "No. I'm not going to use a plane. Too slow. I have a broomstick, remember?"

Nichelle could hardly believe what she was hearing. "I thought you were joking when you mentioned it!" she said.

"No, I wasn't. You'll see it when I get there, and the proof will be in how soon you see me," Mallory said. "Let's get off the phone so I can get to you. I'll see you in a couple of hours."

She explained how to buy the necessary pills from the Silphium Society website.

Nichelle said good-bye and thank you, ended the call, and after a moment of stunned silence, told Jeanne that help would arrive in about two hours.

Jeanne was surprised, but pleased.

They went online, found the link to buy the pills, and Nichelle said, "For the lower-than-a-D&C-cost of $150, they're yours."

Jeanne opened her purse and took out her credit card. She completed the transaction, then looked at her professor, still anxious.

"Where is your niece now?"

"In our room. We did a pregnancy test last night when she said she hadn't gotten her period after six weeks. I made her tell me everything. She cried, watched while I dug the pregnancy test out of my bag, and cried some more when we looked at the pee stick. I gave her some chocolate and told her I'd figure something out."

"Where are your parents and grandmother?"

"They went to settle my brother's estate. They'll be gone for a few days."

They checked on Callie.

Jeanne introduced her professor to her niece.

Nichelle smiled politely and said, "It's nice to meet you."

Callie looked at them both with wide, panicked eyes.

"We've called someone to come and see you," Jeanne told her. "It's a secret. You remember what I told you about the new and horrid laws in Texas, right?"

"Yes." Callie's eyes were large anyway, but her anxiety made them seem huge.

Nichelle said, "We're getting you some help. Those laws don't deserve any respect."

Callie seemed soothed by those words.

Jeanne put the TV on in their room and gave Callie the remote control, and they walked out.

"Let's have a cup of tea and try to relax," Nichelle said in what she hoped was a calming tone.

They made some blueberry lavender tea and watched Jeanne's TV for a while. *Outlander* reruns were on, and Jeanne seemed to relax a bit.

After two episodes had run, they heard a soft knock on the door.

Nichelle looked out the window.

Mallory had arrived.

She had her doctor's bag with her.

And she was in fact carrying a broomstick.

It was purple.

Nichelle opened the door quickly and let her in.

"I should have guessed that your broomstick would be purple!" she said, laughing as she hugged the Wiccan gynecologist.

Mallory grinned, leaned the broomstick against the wall behind the door, and turned to meet Jeanne.

"So, you need and want an abortion."

Jeanne nodded. "Yes. Thank you for coming." She looked back and forth between the broomstick and the medical bag.

Mallory followed her gaze and laughed. "The magical portion of this assistance is over," she said. "That was transportation. The abortion will be done via medical means."

"Oh…!" Jeanne said, nodding. She smiled, then looked serious.

"How far along are you?" Mallory wanted to know.

"Not me. It's my twelve-year-old niece, Callie. She's late for her next period, and we used a pregnancy test. It's positive. I bought it in Louisiana when she called me the night before last, just before I came home."

Nichelle and Mallory exchanged glances.

"That was smart," Nichelle said.

Mallory nodded.

They went into Jeanne and Callie's room and introduced Dr. Moonmist.

Callie shut off the sound on the TV and turned around to look at the doctor.

"I'm going to examine you first, just to confirm it," she said. With that, she proceeded to conduct a more complete patient interview and to check her vital signs with her stethoscope.

"Yup, no doubt about it. You're pregnant."

Callie looked like she would cry again.

"Don't worry," Mallory said, hoping she sounded reassuring. "You soon won't be, and the pregnancy police of this state won't find out. I have the pills you need with me."

She took them out of her medical bag.

"As it so happens," Mallory announced, "I am off for the next couple of days. Willow is feeding my cat. I can stay until this is over, and then fly back at night."

Jeanne and Callie looked so overjoyed to hear this that a group hug ensued.

"What terrific, good luck!" Jeanne said. "What can I do to repay you for all this time away from your home?" she asked, somewhat at a loss.

"Help her recover and move away from forced birther states, that's what," Mallory said. "We'll have to stay here for now. I don't want to be seen by anyone in the area. Secrecy is important for me; it leaves me able to keep helping women."

Jeanne nodded. "I have plenty of food: fruit, vegetarian, chicken, and seafood frozen meals, fresh bread…I stocked up for my professor's visit," she explained.

Callie listened to this exchange.

She was breathing a little easier now.

"I'm impressed!" Mallory said. "Now, Callie, let's get started. Take one of these mifespristone pills now with water."

She did that. It was just after 9 p.m.

"Okay, what next?" the girl asked.

"Try to relax and wait 24 hours. We should probably sleep now. It's late."

Everyone agreed, and the dolls settled onto the sofas and used them as beds.

Callie was told to get into bed, which Jeanne lined with padding, expecting her to bleed soon.

It was a double bed, and Callie wanted Jeanne with her.

Everyone went to sleep.

Well…not immediately.

Mallory got the entire story out of Nichelle first.

Then they went to sleep.

The next day was uneventful.

Callie had decided that she liked *Outlander*. It turned out that she had been watching it in the other room. Therefore, more *Outlander* episodes were watched by all out in the living room.

When 24 hours had passed, Mallory told Callie to put 4 more mifepristone pills under her tongue and let them dissolve for 30 minutes.

Jeanne sat there, glancing at the TV, which had the news on.

The Texas attorney general was on, announcing that he was prosecuting a woman for a miscarriage.

Nichelle changed the channel.

"That is NOT going to happen to you," she said.

Callie nodded, wide-eyed.

Mallory smiled calmly as she watched the patient.

"You're doing fine," she told her.

After 30 minutes, Callie said, "They're not totally dissolved."

Mallory gave her a glass of water.

"One gulp should do it."

It did.

"Now what?" Jeanne asked.

"In 3 hours, with 2 more pills, she'll do this again, and then in another 3 hours, 2 more pills. After that, you'll save the leftover pills in case she needs them, and call me if you think she does. But let's not worry about that just yet."

They had some blueberry lavender tea after about an hour and kept up the *Outlander* marathon to pass the time.

"At least we have plenty of this show to watch," Mallory said. "They've made enough seasons of it."

Jeanne and Nichelle laughed. They were pleased to note that Callie seemed thoroughly engrossed in the story.

The 3-hour interval ended, and Callie took 2 more pills.

She was starting to get cramps.

Mallory said that that was a good thing.

"The pills are working," she added.

She gave Callie 800 mg of ibuprofen for the pain, which meant 4 pills.

Nichelle turned off the television and helped get Callie into bed.

Mallory settled the sofas into place, but picked up a book from Jeanne's shelf. It was John Irving's *The Cider House Rules*, a novel about abortion in Maine in the first half of the twentieth century.

"I'm not going to sleep until the last dose is taken," she told Nichelle.

Nichelle nodded and laid down to rest.

After another 3 hours, it was a little after midnight.

Mallory got up and supervised Callie as she let 2 more pills dissolve in her mouth.

"Okay, that's it. Try to sleep. We're here if you need us," she said, and laid down on her sofa.

Jeanne thanked her as Callie laid back on her pillow.

Mallory didn't expect her to have a relaxing sleep, but had told her to try anyway.

The next day was tougher.

Callie was feeling nauseated, with more intense cramping. She was bleeding heavily.

Suddenly, she felt something larger than a gush of blood and more solid pass out of her and onto the pad she was wearing.

"Let's see it," Mallory said.

Callie went to the bathroom and Mallory followed.

"Okay, congratulations," Mallory told her. "That is the evidence that we needed to remove from you and that we now need to dispose of carefully."

Callie peeled the adhesive pad out of her panties and placed it on the sink counter. She quickly replaced it, then came out of the bathroom.

Jeanne asked, "How will we do that?"

Mallory considered this. It was early evening now. It was starting to get dark.

She glanced around the small house.

No fireplace, of course.

And no curtain over the kitchen sink.

She left the pad in the bathroom, walked over to the kitchen sink, and turned on the hot water.

"The remains must be burned, and in here, not outside where anyone might notice. I'll steam up the window over the kitchen sink while I'm burning the remains."

Nichelle asked, "Jeanne, what are your neighbors like? I did see some MAGA bumper stickers and some other stuff…"

Jeanne replied, "This is rabid anti-abortion MAGA country. My family and I are blue specks in it, so we don't talk outside of the house about this."

"That just confirms my warning about going outside with this," Mallory said. "The window is pretty well steamed up now."

She got the pad, got an herbal sachet from her medical bag, took out her wand, and incinerated the tissue and the herbs behind the steamed-up window, leaving the pad empty of all but blood.

"That ought to do it," she said. "I have to get back. When it gets dark, I'll go."

"Thank you again," Jeanne and Nichelle said.

"Thank you, Dr. Moonmist," Callie said.

"That's what I do," Mallory said. "I'm here to help women, first and foremost. And girls."

Callie smiled.

So did Jeanne and Nichelle.

"You're going to be okay," Mallory said to all of them.

Callie hugged her.

Jeanne turned apologetically to her professor. "I'm really sorry to have taken up so much of your time and visit with this!"

Nichelle waved her off. "Don't let it worry you. My sister is feeding my cat, and I have plenty of time. I was planning on staying in Texas for four days anyway. It only takes an hour or so to go over your grant and file the rest of the details online. And we did that yesterday, after lunch."

Jeanne looked relieved.

Mallory watched them, happy to see life going on as normal for Callie.

"If you feel up to going for a walk, I recommend it," she told her.

Callie looked up, considering that. "Will that help with the cramps?"

Mallory nodded.

"Professor, I could take you to the River Walk. It's really pretty, and Callie likes the shops and restaurants and cafés along that area. I don't know if she's up to visiting the Alamo, but we could definitely enjoy the rest of that area."

Nichelle smiled. "Callie, only if you're feeling up to it. Otherwise, we'll come back here and you can rest."

Callie smiled. "Okay. Thanks!"

Mallory stayed for another dinner, with black raspberry chocolate chip yoghurt bars for dessert.

After about an hour, it was dark.

Callie was feeling okay. The bleeding was heavy, like a menstrual period, but the other discomfort was easing. She had eaten a light meal, which helped.

Mallory packed her bag, which didn't look too obviously like a medical one, Nichelle noted. It was embroidered with a purple heart shape.

Mallory saw her scrutinizing it and said, "I did that. I didn't want to go on clandestine visits with a cross or a Caduseus emblazoned on this bag."

"Smart," Nichelle said, nodding.

Mallory shouldered the bag, picked up her purple broomstick and looked out through the curtains.

Some lights in other trailers were on, but the curtains were drawn.

Nevertheless, Mallory took out her wand and said a few spells before stepping outside.

"One can't be too careful," she said. "It was lovely to meet you, Jeanne and Callie, and lovely to see you again, Nichelle."

Mallory then opened the door, stepped onto the grass, straddled the broomstick, and took off into the darkness.

Nichelle and Jeanne did take Callie out for that walk the next day, and with a few pauses for rest room use, they had a cheerful stroll in downtown San Antonio.

Callie asked Jeanne if she could live with her after she got her Ph.D.

"That's my plan," Jeanne told her. "We're going to a pro-choice state. There are still lots of them."

Nichelle fervently hoped that that would continue to be so, but said nothing.

"Stephen Colbert's show has been cancelled," Antoinette said as she and Manon were shown to their table.

She was very angry and depressed about it.

"He's up for an Emmy award, along with the other late-night comedians, all of whom enjoy reaming Herr Pumpkingropenfuhrer relentlessly."

Manon looked sympathetic, and interested.

"He's your favorite, isn't he?" she asked.

"Yes. I hope he wins, and not just because he's the best one in terms of research, political, social, economic, and cultural interviews with such guests, and his cooking segments. I want him to win as a slap in the face to the Pumpkingropenfuhrer."

"That would be nice," Manon said.

They looked at the menus, and decided to share an order of baba ghanoush. They each ordered chilled curried carrot soup and chicken curry over basmati rice, put down the menus, and resumed their conversation.

"Wasn't he demanding that Colbert's show be cancelled just so that he wouldn't have to endure any further criticism by him?" Manon asked.

"He was," Antoinette confirmed. "This is the epitome of fascism. He's angry about an interview that CBS's *60 Minutes* did with his opponent – who mopped the floor with him in their presidential debate – and would not approve a financial merger between CBS's owner, Paramount, and Skydance movie corporation, unless *The Late Show with Stephen Colbert* was cancelled."

Manon was outraged. "That really is fascism," she said. "Why is history repeating itself?!"

"Overpopulation strains resources, which brings out the worst behavior in many humans, including voting behavior," Antoinette said. "That, and collective human memory, for people who are not students of history, only lasts ninety years."

Manon was aghast. "I did not know that…"

"Now they're pushing legislation that claims that women shouldn't have abortion medications because when they pee after taking it, it gets in the water supply!" Antoinette was on a roll of a tirade.

"Flushing pills puts your prescription drugs in the water supply even more directly, and that can't be filtered out, either," Manon said, "so that's just ridiculous."

"I told my older cousin about that, and he looked guilty but didn't say anything. Shortly after that, I was in the kitchen and noticed his prescription bottles, empty, in the recycle bin and the expired pills in the garbage can."

"And you knew he did that…" Manon said, smiling.

"To quote Bill Maher, 'I don't know it for a fact; I just know it's true,'" Antoinette said.

Manon nodded in agreement.

The server arrived with their appetizer.

As they dipped into the baba ghanoush, the huge flatscreen TV on the wall above the bar, which was tuned in to MSNBC, was running a story that caught their attention.

Katy Tur was talking about a mysterious helper of women in anti-abortion states. No one had seen this person – well, no one who would describe her.

Antoinette and Manon stopped chewing to stare at each other with a fiery gleam in their eyes. Then they turned back to watch the report.

"Attorneys general and police in Texas, Louisiana, and North Dakota are seeking information as to who this is, where they are based, and how they operate."

Tur continued, "But the women whose health has been safeguarded aren't talking, and their physicians have no records of treating them. Further complicating any efforts to prosecute anyone is the fact that no supplies that might have been used to treat the women are unaccounted for."

The soup arrived, garnished with fresh snipped chives and nasturtiums.

They ate it in silence, their attention riveted on the news story.

Katy Tur was smiling as she talked.

So were the dolls as they listened to her.

Antoinette's mood had lifted considerably.

Manon smiled at her briefly.

Tur concluded with: "Whoever this is, from women everywhere, both in states that accept that we are full human beings with autonomy and agency over our own bodies and in anti-abortion states, thank you very much for what you are doing."

"You're welcome," Antoinette whispered, looking down at her dish.

The server had just switched their empty soup bowls for ones with chicken curry garnished with fresh chives from the local farmers' market.

Violin Auction at Christie's

It was a nice day for an auction – rainy and busy.

The auction that afternoon was to include a set of four rare tapestries that had recently been found and restored in a remote chateau in France, and three very special violins. (Their wealthy owners had recently died, and their estates were selling them.)

Manon was very excited about all this.

No, that was putting it mildly.

Manon was in her element, and on cloud nine.

She knew the particulars of these lots in minute detail, but just to be sure of generating as much enthusiasm as possible, she had invited Antoinette to work the room with her.

Well…she hadn't put it like that, but Antoinette was happy to oblige her.

The dolls came in from the rain and stopped in Manon's office to leave their coats.

Manon was also still jubilant about Lilith's coup with the birth control pills. "She really outdid herself," Manon said. "The news is still full of reports about people in sub-Saharan Africa benefitting from having them."

"That was so great to hear about," Antoinette said. "But if we do our job right, most of it will all be unnoticed and unreported. That couldn't be, but most of the other work can."

They paused to look at each other's dresses.

The two of them had had their couturière outfit them for this occasion, in patterns that depicted the backgrounds of famous French tapestries. Antoinette wore a Millefleur background, while Manon wore the Unicorn in Captivity one.

"Perfect!" Manon said.

Antoinette grinned, and they went out into the gallery.

It was already half-full of people, and the buzz of conversations in the high-ceilinged room made it feel overstimulating for Antoinette.

As a person on the autism spectrum, she tended to avoid getting too close to large groups. The noise and intensity bothered her.

On stage, she had her own space, and the groups got quiet, to hear her play. Oh well…she could manage for an hour or so until the bidding started, which would be in another room.

Manon knew this, so she smiled and let
Antoinette look at each tapestry and then the violins.
Having a chance to see the items would put her at

ease. It was better than having to start by meeting and interacting with people.

They saw Ileandra at the other end of the room.

The alien gave them a slight smile and nodded.

They nodded back, leaving her, as planned, to try to talk to people on her own.

"I hope she does okay, outing herself," Antoinette said to Manon, in an undertone.

"I hope so too," Manon replied.

No one heard them.

The tapestries were gorgeous. They each had a pale blue background, with other hues, and depicted landscapes with pastoral scenes of Medieval aristocrats milling about…and dragons.

"Huh…no unicorns," Antoinette said.

Manon laughed. "No. But dragons are fun."

"Yes, they are," Antoinette replied.

She quickly moved around the perimeter of the room, taking in the set of tapestries, admiring them. Then she turned to the free-standing pedestals with glass boxes on top that showcased the violins.

Manon watched her, staying nearby.

Antoinette was quite a sight to behold: a famous violinist with her ever-present, 1680s Stradivarius violin, inspecting other priceless violins.

Nevertheless, prices would soon be put on them.

Once paired with a violinist who was worthy of it, a rare violin was constantly carried by its player. This was part of the responsibility of having the honor to play it.

Antoinette was happy to guard her instrument; it was her constant companion because she loved to make it sing, and could do so with the loveliest, most mellifluous tones, just as the luthier crafted it to make. She composed her own tunes with it, too.

She moved closer to inspect a violin.

It was not a Stradivarius.

It was an Amati.

Nicolò Amati was thought of as the best luthier of his family. He crafted violins from the 1620s until his death in 1684, including this one.

"What is it like to play one of Amati's violins?" Manon asked, genuinely curious. Reading about it was just not the same as hearing a violinist of Antoinette's calibre describe it.

"It's definitely different," Antoinette said. "Both Amati and Stradivarius violins have their own qualities. They offer different sounds."

Around the famous violinist, groups of people fell quiet, listening.

If Antoinette noticed, she gave no sign.

She continued, "An Amati is quieter. It has a smaller body than later violins. It sounds sweet and warm. It is suitable for chamber music, though the preference for this luthier's violins over those of his supposed apprentice is really just a matter of taste."

Manon let her go on, because this was exactly the presentation she had hoped for. It meant much more to the buyers coming from a violinist than from a curator.

Soon someone to her left spoke up.

"Why do you say 'supposed' apprentice? Did Antoinio Stradivarius study under him?"

It was a man Manon had encountered before. He was an investor with Blackstone Inc. That firm handled more than $1 trillion in assets. She had worked with several wealthy people whose money was handled by it.

Antoinette knew none of this; Manon would tell her that later. Meanwhile, she calmly replied to him, "There is scant evidence that Antonio Stradivarius actually studied with Nicolò Amati. All there is to support that idea is one label, which he affixed to his 1666 violin. Unlike other people, he didn't usually bother with labels. So, we can't be sure one way or the other. It's possible, but not certain."

"Oh…" the man said, nodding.

Funny how people will just accept as an absolute truth what an illustrious violinist says, Manon thought to herself. If she, a curator had said this, a debate and lengthy discussion would have ensued. The contrast amused her.

But this was what she had wanted: for Antoinette to say these things, so that people would simply take in the information and focus on the merchandise.

Antoinette turned around to look at the next violin, which had been made by Stradivarius. It was made in the 1660s, but it was not the 1666 one; it had been crafted a couple of years later.

"What is the sound of a Stradivarius violin like, compared with that of an Amati?" a woman asked.

She was elegantly dressed, and could have stepped out of a page from *Town & Country* magazine. Manon had sold her husband the ring, earrings, pin, and necklace she was wearing, each on separate occasions.

Antoinette knew that the woman was hoping she would play a few notes, but for the moment, she just smiled and said a few more facts about violins. It wasn't time to show off…not just yet.

"A Stradivarius sounds a bit different, naturally. It has a deeper tone, which projects more. That is what makes it more popular for big concert halls, because that makes it acoustically easier to appreciate. The difference is partly due to the fact that, by the time Strads were being crafted, the art of doing so had been more developed. Also, the ones he crafted later on, in the 18th century, were larger than any of the ones you see here."

A chorus of "Oh…." responded to that as her listeners absorbed this.

"Stradivarius is famous for the exceptionally brilliant, deep tones of his instruments," Antoinette said, walking over to see the last of the violins.

This one was crafted in the 1690s. Like the other two Strads in the room (including Antoinette's), it had a deep, dark-red hue to it that others lacked. It was this detail that made it easy to spot one on an orchestral stage.

"These are all exceptional instruments," Antoinette said. "Any violinist would be very lucky to have one."

Nods all around the group, which had grown.

At this point, most of the people in the room were watching Antoinette and listening to what she had to say about each violin. Eyes moved back and forth between her and the ones encased in glass.

With a devilish gleam in her eyes, Antoinette smiled and raised her own Stradivarius to her chin, and lifted the bow to its strings.

She played a few notes, just to demonstrate the timbre and deep sound of her instrument. The tune was Niccolò Paganini's Caprice No. 24.

Manon nodded at her to go ahead and play it through, so she did.

If it would help her friend, Antoinette was willing to show off a bit. But just a little bit. The bidding was to commence in a little while, and this was not a free concert. It was just a taste – a teaser – to make her listeners want more…and buy a rare violin.

When she finished, the room erupted in applause.

Antoinette smiled, bowed, and put her violin back in its usual position to indicate that that was all she would play.

People smiled, some said, "Thank you!" with sincere sounds of appreciation, and then they turned to look at the violins on display, leaving her to chat with just a few hangers-on.

Someone wanted to know more about Antoinette's violin, so she told the small remaining group of people that it was made in the 1680s, and that she had bought it several years ago.

Manon knew the full details: Antoinette, once she had become wealthy enough on her own from giving many concerts, had bought it from her benefactor. That benefactor was a wealthy woman that her grandmother had known, now both deceased.

Today, however, the dolls would watch as the wealthy bidders who were at Christie's vied to become such benefactors.

Once they were the proud owners of an Amati or a Stradivarius, they would buy insurance policies for the instruments and approach another virtuoso violinist to pair it with.

Or not; the Amati could end up in a museum.

Amatis were fewer in number, and thus rarer.

There was also the issue of their sweet, quieter tone, so it was anyone's guess what would become of that instrument.

As it turned out, Antoinette and Manon had guessed correctly: the Amati ended up at the Boston Museum of Fine Arts.

The Strads, however, went to some fine young people whom Antoinette had met when she had judged them in competitions at Juilliard and at the Curtis Institute in Philadelphia.

Ileandra Confronts Disbelief

Ileandra was having a frustrating time.

She had thought it would be easier to introduce herself as an alien from another planet that orbits another star – from another solar system – but it hadn't been.

People just didn't believe her.

She was with Manon and Antoinette at Christie's auction house in Manhattan.

Not wanting to cause any problems for them, she was keeping her distance from them. She had arrived separately, and had not gone to stand with them.

This was Manon's place of work, after all, and Antoinette was there to help her by chatting up wealthy patrons of the musical arts about the violins. The idea was that these wealthy attendees would buy the violins and then lend them to famous talented violinists like Antoinette.

It was a matter of prestige for the artists' patrons, and a crucial career opportunity for young virtuoso violinists, who would have to give many more concerts before they could afford to own a Stradivarius or an Amati violin.

The alien was therefore not going to let the people she was interacting with see that they knew her while outing herself as such.

Ileandra knew that outing herself as an extra-terrestrial came with the risk that she would simply be written off as a crazy person.

She wanted to stay and observe people, and keep her freedom, not get carted away by the police or some mental institution employees in white coats.

After a few attempts, she decided that it wasn't working out very well and retreated to a corner with her mocktail of fruit juice and wine cooler.

She looked so dejected that an older man approached her and stood next to her. She glanced up at him.

"I believe you," he said. "I'm a retired neurologist. I can see that you are physiologically a bit different from humans. But I'm afraid that my belief is all I can give you; if I announce it to the room, I'll be written off as a senile old man."

Ileandra nodded. "Thank you for that," she said to him. She felt a bit better about it after that.

Hospital Bewitchment

A brain-dead woman in Georgia was pregnant.

The hospital that she had been brought to was keeping her on life support even though she had told her husband that she didn't want that – not even if she was pregnant. How could a feeding tube possibly give a fetus a strong, healthy body to start its life with after birth?! She had said all that to him.

They hadn't thought about it further until a drunk driver hit their car one evening as they drove home from a dinner date. The woman was brain-dead on impact.

Her pregnancy, just over six weeks along, hadn't even been detected until she arrived at the hospital.

Now, against her will, her husband's will, and that of her parents, the hospital was keeping her body alive as an incubator.

Mallory had been following the news for patients who needed help but also couldn't ask for it. This could be a detailed task, involving a lot of reading and listening to understand individual cases.

What did the patient want?

That was the question she wanted resolved before she took any action. It was what mattered to her most as a healthcare practitioner: bodily autonomy for the patient above all else.

Her patients just happened to all be female.

Sometimes, to answer this question when the patient was brain-dead due to an accident or sudden illness, the data came from her relatives. If she was lucky, the patient had left a do-not-resuscitate order.

But most of the women who were in that situation, brain-dead but pregnant, had not, because they were young and had thought that they had plenty of time left to live and make a will.

Thus, Mallory and the rest of the nation had watched before this as another woman, a young nurse and mother of a little boy in Georgia, pregnant, had become a brain-dead patient at a hospital in a state where abortion had been made illegal after the fall of *Roe v. Wade*.

The fetus had been delivered via Caesarean section weighing 2 pounds and gone directly to the neonatal intensive care unit (NICU). The family was stuck with the bills, which were in the tens of thousands of dollars per day.

Georgia had passed this law in 2019, three years before the *Dobbs* ruling. It banned any abortion after a fetal heartbeat could be detected, which is at 6 weeks – before a woman knows she is pregnant. Brain activity comes later on for a fetus, at 8 weeks.

Viability outside the uterus comes after 24 weeks.

That's 5 and a half months.

That is the point in a human pregnancy that the *Roe v. Wade* world had deemed to be the cutoff point for abortions.

That was plenty of time for a woman to know she was pregnant and decide whether or not to remain so.

But laws such as Georgia's, which had to remain dormant until the *Dobbs* ruling, were forced birther laws. They meant to take that decision away from women.

So…here was another case of a woman's corpse being treated as an incubator.

"I guess no one ever thought of applying laws about desecrating a corpse to these cases," Mallory said angrily as she watched the news.

She was in the hospital in Manhattan, on rounds.

During a break, when she had paused for dinner with a cup of coffee at the cafeteria, she saw this report of the woman who had essentially died in a car crash but was trapped on life support for a pregnancy that she had not even known about.

Her boyfriend sat with her, watching.

At least he didn't have to deal with such problems as a psychiatrist – only the emotional trauma afterward. Bad enough, but that wouldn't involve legal problems. Of course, she wanted someone who didn't have to worry about the same risks that she did. And she could trust him.

"I'm off in a couple of hours," Mallory said, glancing up at the TV and then back at her food. She picked at her salad and grilled cheese sandwich – pepperjack on whole wheat. "At least I'm dressed for the occasion."

The boyfriend just said, "I'll feed Maleficent."

She smiled at him and said, "Thank you."

She finished her strawberry-mango smoothie and they went back to work. She would need the calories she had just consumed for what she would do.

The rest of Mallory's rounds were uneventful, and she was glad. She briefed the next physician on her cases and left.

After a quick trip to the locker room to freshen up, she opened her locker and took out her purple broomstick.

It was enchanted so that no one would notice it.

Mallory had been bringing it to the hospital since the end of *Roe v. Wade*, but until Antoinette had founded the Silphium Society, she had felt lost and unsure of how keeping it on hand at all times would help her to help anyone.

No more.

She climbed the staircase to the roof.

There was no helipad with helicopter pilots to worry about; the cluster of hospitals where she worked was on east 68th Street. It shared use of the helipad for Columbia University's Irving Medical Center at West 181st Street.

There were some maintenance people on the roof, but Mallory wasn't concerned.

They could only see her, not her broomstick.

She smiled and waved, and went around the other side of the array of generators. There were clusters of them here and there atop each wing of the buildings.

With no one paying direct attention to her, she stepped astride her broomstick and took off into the night, over the city, and turned toward Emory University Hospital in Atlanta, Georgia.

It was a beautiful, warm, clear night.

After briefly admiring the view of the city lights below her, Mallory took off at the broomstick's top speed.

The trip took her just a quarter of an hour.

She was in a hurry; this was a covert op.

As she was on her final approach to the hospital, she remembered seeing, on Google Maps, that there was a grassy area in front of its main building with some leafy trees. Perfect.

She landed, chose one of them, and levitated her broomstick up one of them. It looked healthy, and wasn't touching any electrical wires. She made the broomstick cling to the bark, where it would wait for her, unnoticed and enchanted.

Great!

Time to go into the hospital and see the patient.

Mallory walked out of the trees and through the doors of the hospital. No one stopped her as she headed for the ICU ward. Her spells were working.

This was the riskiest thing she had done thus far.

Her plan was to jinx all closed-circuit cameras from entry to exit. No recordings of her face could be made.

What about her face? Some people had excellent memories for faces. More jinxes – for memories. She would cloud them.

Her wand? Another jinx; people glancing in her direction would be convinced that she carried a stethoscope.

It took a lot of concentration to keep this up, but Mallory was determined.

She looked up the woman's name in the hospital logs. Good…she was on the right floor, in the right ward…and the room the patient was in was just down the hall.

Mallory walked in as if she belonged there.

It always helped to convince people that you belonged somewhere if you acted like it. They could realize that you didn't later, when you were long gone…

Mallory was at the foot of the brain-dead woman's bed.

Feeding tubes were hooked up to her body.

Monitors tracked her vital signs.

Mallory knew that the moment the patient's body died, the machines would make a loud, screech of a sound that would bring the staff running.

She thought that over.

A couple of carefully thought-out spells would deal with that: one for the sounds, and the other for what the staff saw on the monitors — both in here and out at the nurses' station.

There. Done.

That was it.

Mallory paused to look at the woman's face.

"I'm sorry that the laws in Georgia don't respect you," she said to her. Perhaps the woman's ghost was listening, as she hoped. "The laws of slavery didn't respect slaves, so we won't show law that deny women our bodily autonomy any respect, either."

With that, Mallory took out her wand and induced the patient's uterus to expel its contents, embryo and all.

A bloody stain soon spread across the bed.
Mallory checked the body; the embryo was out.
Good. Her job was done…almost.
She had to get out of here unnoticed.
Glancing up and down the hallway, Mallory decided to check a couple of other patients on her way out, just for show.
As she did so, she cast another spell – a strong one – bewitching the hospital staff to not notice for over half an hour…too late to do anything about it!
Soon she was back outside, calmly walking up to that tree and levitating her broomstick down.
She hopped on and kicked off into the night.
Georgia was pretty, Mallory mused to herself.
Too bad it was so hostile to women of reproductive age. It would probably lead to some serious brain drain as both doctors and potential patients moved to friendlier states.
Back home with her cat, she put her broomstick away and kissed her boyfriend.
She made a cup of rose and hibiscus tea and turned on the TV.
There it was: breaking news of the condition of her Georgia patient.
The hospital staff had checked on her, founded that the embryonic tissue was out of her, and pulled the plugs on her life support equipment and feeding tubes.
The widower was crying quietly but coherent.
He said he was grateful that his wife's time in the hospital was over. "This was not how she wanted it,

but it's the closest thing to it. I don't know how it happened, but I'm glad it did."

Forced birther lawmakers, however, were raging at the hospital and demanding a full investigation.

"Good luck," Mallory said, mocking them. "You won't get answers. And you didn't get to force your views and wishes on that woman and her family."

The physicians at Emory University Hospital said that once a uterus expels its contents, there is no going back. It just happened sometimes, as a natural response. It was a miscarriage that had happened in a hospital setting, and no one's fault.

Mallory's boyfriend had a few words to say about the hospital bills. "Those lawmakers should have to pay the costs of keeping brain-dead women alive as incubators."

The two of them sat down with the cat and watched the news, alternating between laughter and anger at the running commentary by forced birthers who were interviewed, including lawmakers and anti-abortion activists, until *The Late Show with Stephen Colbert* began.

"He'll comment on this tomorrow," Mallory said. The show was pre-recorded. This episode wouldn't even mention this case.

The comedian's humor calmed them down and relaxed them, and soon they were ready to sleep. They slept very well, and quite soundly.

Data Rescue

Willow and Lilith sat in front of their computers at the Silphium Society's temporary office, backing up data.

This was another aspect of the public face of the Silphium Society: copies of websites that had been taken offline by the fascists were being made and saved in various locations around the country.

The idea was that it would be far easier to repair the damage when the time came to do so with this data saved. Having it in more than one place guaranteed extra security for it.

They were in Willow's Manhattan apartment, which she shared with her American husband and their cat, Eleanore.

"There is nothing that the one that Antoinette calls Herr Pumpkingropenfuhrer hates like an informed and educated electorate," Lilith said as she saved the data. "He doesn't want journalists or independent education."

Willow was listening to her as she worked. She had been shown what to do, and was busy doing the same thing. She let Lilith vent.

Lilith went on, "Antoinette has plans to fund what has been stripped of funding. She can't and won't be doing it all by herself; she may be wealthy, but she won't stay that way and be able to help if she doesn't get more help. Manon and I are going to get that for her."

Willow nodded. She knew all about the fundraising plans, but the details of getting specific individuals with deep bank accounts were up to them. She and Lilith would set up the accounts, endowments, and whatever other financial arrangements that were needed to do all this.

The data that they were working to back up was being saved in cooperation and coordination with an effort that was based in California. It was called the Internet Archive, and it had been designated as a Federal Depository Library by one of that state's senators.

Its founder and digital librarian, Brewster Kahle, needed lots of people to help, and the Silphium Society had volunteered its services.

After they had finished their work, they got ready to leave. They were meeting Antoinette to look at another apartment, which she had bought as official office space for the Silphium Society.

Willow put on her coat; it was misty out.

They found Manon in the premises when they arrived. Manon was determined to help with the Silphium Society, so she was busy setting up the furniture, coffee machine, refrigerator, and desktop computers.

She was wearing a beautiful outfit. It was for an event that evening at Christie's auction house. Illuminated manuscripts were being shown, and the pattern of her dress depicted the illustrations from a calligraphy book, which is what illuminations are.

This particular pattern was from a manuscript called the *Mira calligraphiae monumenta*. This is a book made of vellum (animal skin that has been scraped).

Its name translates to *The Model Book of Calligraphy* and it was created for the Holy Roman Emperor Ferdinand I from 1561-1562. It shows an immense range of scripts that calligraphers could use, which the artist and the emperor didn't want forgotten due to the advent of the printing press.

Thirty years later, his grandson, Rudolph II, had the manuscript illuminated. It is kept at the Getty Center in Los Angeles, California.

Willow and Lilith spent a few minutes looking at Manon's dress and admiring it, exclaiming over the gorgeous floral parts of the pattern, the curls of ribbon, and the huge honeybees.

When they were done looking at it, Manon presented them with them a treat that she had made for them to enjoy at the new office: raspberry Linzer heart cookies.

Lilith and Mallory were delighted!

The cookies tasted wonderful, which came as no surprise. The dolls enjoyed the cookies for a little while, and then Manon left for work at Christie's auction house.

Professor, Look!

Nichelle was having a great time snorkeling.

She and the graduate students were moored off the coast of Cancun, Mexico, midway between it and Cuba.

It has been a busy day.

To start with, a seal had surprised everyone while they were finishing their coffee. It was at the end of breakfast, so some of the students were cleaning up, washing the dishes in the gallery, so they missed the amazing sight of it climbing the metal ladder.

Everyone had rushed to the deck to see it.

The seal moved quickly to a pile of rope to the right of the ladder and turned to face the humans, barking earnestly at them.

Nichelle warned them all not to overwhelm the seal with attention; just stay at a discreet distance and watch.

"It's female," she said, looking carefully at the seal. "And she's injured."

The seal had a bloody gash on the side of her neck, which looked deep and painful.

Nichelle, talking quietly to the seal, approached her. "Don't worry, we're going to help you," she said, and looked at the gash.

The seal turned her head so that Nichelle could get a better look at her injury.

Then it barked at her, as if to ask for help.

"You're in luck," Nichelle said. "I know you want this injury treated by a human veterinarian. That's me. You found me," she added, smiling.

The seal looked at her, listening.

Nichelle was sure that seals and other creatures understood humans, and that they were as intelligent as we are. Just because a life form can't talk the same way that humans can doesn't mean that they don't understand us.

Andreas, a student from Greece, brought her medical bag to her. She opened it, laid out all of the tools that she needed, and turned to the seal.

She looked at Nichelle and the threaded suture needle, then at the syringe in Nichelle's hand.

"I'm going to give you a drug that will keep you from feeling it while I stitch up that wound," she told the seal. But first, you will feel a sting as I give it to you. It's the best I can do to keep this from hurting you a lot more."

The seal listened, watching her every move.

She didn't know how much it understood, but she had to proceed, so she walked up to the seal and placed the syringe on her neck.

"Ready? I'm going to inject the drug now," she said. She didn't use the word 'anaesthesia' deliberately. This was healthcare, not a vocabulary test.

The seal let her do the deed!

Nichelle smiled and said, "You did very well. We'll just wait a minute or so for that to take effect, and then I will stitch you up. Meanwhile, I'm going to clean the wound."

She swabbed it thoroughly with disinfectant.

The seal didn't even flinch, so she reached for the suture needle.

She smiled again at her. "I'm going to stitch you up now. Please try to hold still."

The seal regarded her calmly as she said this, so Nichelle went ahead with the job. It took ten stitches.

She tied the thread and cut it.

"Those sutures will dissolve in several days, so you won't have to come back. You're all set," she told the seal.

The seal barked at her once, and it seemed to be thanking her.

She smiled and stood up.

Everyone watched as the seal went over to the ladder and jumped back into the water. It swam off, and that was that.

Shondra, a graduate student in her twenties who wanted to go to veterinary school and follow her professor's career path, was elated. "That was terrific!" she said, grinning from ear to ear. "She seemed to understand you perfectly."

Nichelle smiled back. "The important thing is to go slowly, and explain everything to the creature. Never assume that they don't understand. They don't have to understand the way we do, word for word. They just have to have time to take in what we are doing and draw their own conclusions. Of course, if the creature is so badly injured that we work on them under total anaesthesia, we can just do the deed without that. But for local anaesthesia, what you just saw is what they need."

With that, everyone went back to their usual routine, taking water samples, scuba diving, etc.

Nichelle didn't go yet; her rule was that only half of them could go at any one time, and there were six people on the *Yemoja*, herself and five graduate students.

Lunchtime passed without incident, but you never know whether you will have an uneventful day or a busy one.

Today proved to be a busy day.

Diego came back to the boat about half an hour after lunch, excited. "I found a sea turtle – a huge Kemp's ridley turtle – with a clear plastic straw stuck up its nostril!"

Nichelle asked, "Where is it now?"

"Leah is next to it, over there." He pointed to a spot about fifteen feet away, off to the left. Leah waved and pointed to her right at it.

"I see it. Can you bring it to the boat and get it up here on deck?"

"Sure!" Diego took off.

Soon the enormous, critically endangered turtle was on deck. It was a fascinating creature to look at. It was 30 inches long and must have weighed at least 100 pounds; both Diego and Andreas had hefted it to the deck with Leah's help, pushing from the rear up the boat's ladder.

Sure enough, a huge plastic straw was sticking out of its left nostril. It looked like it was stuck halfway in.

Jeanne brought the medical kit this time.

All Nichelle needed was a pair of strong tweezers.

There was a lot of apologizing to the sea turtle.

"I'm so sorry this happened to you," Nichelle said. "This may hurt, but you need to be rid of this straw."

She tugged at it gently with the tweezers tightly gripped on it, close to the turtle's nostril. It didn't move much. This was going to be a slow and very uncomfortable – for the turtle – process of removal.

It took Nichelle twenty minutes.

She had had the turtle put up on a bench, and she had pulled a chair over to it. She pulled and pulled, gently drawing it out as straight as possible.

Blood ran out of the turtle's nostril.

Nichelle felt sorry for the turtle, but finishing the job was the best thing for it.

After what felt like an interminable amount of time, though, it suddenly came out, all crumpled, gnarled, and nasty-looking.

She sat there, staring at it for an instant, then showed it to the turtle, who looked at it with dislike.

The students took this in.

Leah, Jeanne, and Shonda had been stroking its front feet and the top of its head as Nichelle worked. They stepped back once the job was done, though.

Nichelle wiped at the blood. It had stopped.

The turtle was going to be fine.

The male students cheered, not too loudly so as not to freak the turtle out. Then they looked at Nichelle, who nodded and said, "It can leave now."

They carried it back to the ladder and let it go.

It swam off immediately, and something about the way it moved told them it was happy.

"Okay, my turn to go scuba diving," Nichelle said, getting up and heading below deck to change.

She put on her wet suit and brought out her gear.

At last, a chance to explore more of the Gulf of Mexico. (It would always be that to her and her students — never mind Google Maps' acquiescence to the idiocy of renaming it!) Actually, they were on the edge of the Caribbean Sea, not far from Cancún.

Nichelle climbed down the ladder, put the headgear in place with her mask and breathing tube, and took off, hoping to find the Underwater Museum, also known as the MUSA (Subacuatic Museum of Art).

She found it rather quickly, and pleased to have the chance to swim among the coral-encrusted statues of humans that an artist had affixed to the floor of the gulf.

She saw a circle of statues holding hands and facing out, statues of banksters and corporatists with their heads stuck in the sand, and statues with arms stretched out that grew into tree branches.

Part of the purpose of this art installation was to give coral a place to grow, which was a great success.

The other part was about depicting different aspects of human life that were linked to ocean health, ocean pollution, and climate change.

Plastic, in varying states of decay, plus some that looked freshly dumped into the sea, floated all around her.

It annoyed her no end that this stuff was there.

She swam around, looking at everything for half an hour or so, collecting plastic, photographing it with her underwater camera, and taking samples of coral and seaweed.

It was fun to be out there. Sunshine went through the water, illuminating everything, and the water was a comfortable temperature. She felt a bit cooler in it than she had on her boat.

Suddenly, she saw a huge gray-blue shape up close. A dolphin! It looked at her, then away.

A moment later, it was joined by perhaps fifteen more of them. They surrounded her.

Nichelle put everything away immediately, and it was a good thing she did, because they began to butt her with their noses, not too hard, but enough that she could feel a push.

They were all pushing her in the same direction: they wanted her to go back to her boat.

'Why, though?' she wondered.

But she did it.

She knew when to take sea creatures seriously.

She got to the ladder, climbed up, and pulled the headgear off immediately.

Her students were all pointing behind her and shouting, "Professor, look!"

She looked back and saw it: a fin.

The dolphins had been warning her away from a shark.

Yes, it had definitely been an eventful day.

Paris: Lunch Meeting

Antoinette and Manon were spending some time in Paris. Antoinette had a concert to give, and Manon needed to do some work at the Louvre.

Willow would meet them in a day or so, to coordinate events on Antoinette's musical calendar. She was just arranging some last-minute details for upcoming concerts.

Their fiancés had come along, which meant that their cats didn't have their usual caregivers. But not to worry: Ileandra had volunteered to take care of both Specter and Dauphine at Antoinette's house in Avon, Connecticut.

The plants that they ordered for her were starting to be delivered, so this all worked out perfectly. Ileandra could ferry them out to the backyard at night, have the plants and herself beamed up to the ship, and come back after a few hours to stay with the cats.

Accordingly, everyone: cats, dolls, and fiancés, first went to Connecticut to settle Ileandra and the cats into the house with plenty of food. The alien also had Antoinette's mother's phone number, just in case.

Once the group was settled in Paris, they had a day to relax before getting down to the business of working with the Paris Opéra and at the Louvre.

The fiancés went off to the Musée d'Orsay.

Antoinette and Manon decided to celebrate their two weeks in Paris by going out to lunch together.

"Where shall we go for lunch?" Manon asked. She had no particular place in mind.

Wandering around Paris meant that finding a delightful place to eat was no effort at all. Cafés, bistros, and restaurants of the highest quality were everywhere, offering French cuisine of all types, plus some from other cultures.

Antoinette, of course, wanted French food. As a New Yorker, she could try the food of other cultures there any time. "I would like to eat at the Restaurant Le Soufflé," she said.

Manon knew it; it was located between La Place Vendôme and the Jardin des Tuileries, which abuts the Louvre. "I've never eaten there, but I have heard that its chefs are great artists of taste and presentation," she replied. "Let's go."

Le Soufflé was a beautiful restaurant, with its wood-paned exterior painted a nice shade of light blue. A large upper panel on the front door depicted a waiter from the late 18th century, carrying a tall soufflé held high on a platter.

Le Palais Garnier was in the 9th arrondissement (le neuvième, to the French). The Avenue de l'Opéra goes diagonally southeast from the front entrance of Le Palais Garnier to the Louvre, in the 1ier arrondissement. Between them was La Place Vendôme.

La Place Vendôme was a famous square. It is surrounded by hotels, shops, and upscale restaurants. Antoinette and her fiancé were staying in one of these hotels, called the Hôtel de Vendôme. It has five rooms and 10 suites.

They had the Astronomy Suite. Antoinette's fiancé was delighted when he realized that she had chosen it as a surprise for him!

A suite may be a bit expensive, but it was ideal for Antoinette to practice her violin before going out for the day…and she could afford it.

Manon had an appartement in the area.

It was convenient to her work at the Louvre, where she coordinated finds of rare art, ensuring that they were paired with the ideal spot in that museum, or offered for sale in one of Christie's venues around the world.

The Louvre had the largest collection of art in the world. The proceeds of any sale facilitated by Manon or any other curator working with Christie's auction house go to support its cultural and educational programs.

But back to the Restaurant Le Soufflé.

It would not be fair to deny the reader a description of the delightful meal that Antoinette and Manon enjoyed there.

"It looks so modern inside!" Antoinette remarked as they walked in.

Manon smiled. "Lots of places in Paris do. You see an exterior with a façade that blends in with the area around it, but inside, all bets are off. The décor can be whatever the owners want it to be."

They were shown to a table near the windows, to the left, and handed menus on pretty parchment paper with a serif font.

"What looks good to you?" Manon asked.

"Lots of things!" Antoinette said. "But I can't eat here without having soufflé for every course of the meal," she said with a grin. "It just wouldn't make any sense."

Manon laughed; she agreed.

For the starter course, Manon had the duo de soupe à l'oignon & petit soufflé fromage (small French onion soup & small cheese souffle); Antoinette had a millefeuille de betteraves rouges au chèvre frais & petit soufflé chèvre romarin (millefeuille with beets, goat cheese & small goat cheese, and a rosemary soufflé). A millefeuille is a savory pastry.

Next, for entrées, Antoinette chose the soufflé saumon, ricotta & aneth (salmon, ricotta cheese & dill soufflé); Manon chose the soufflé Henri IV avec sauce volaille aux champignons (cheese soufflé with chicken & mushrooms sauce).

They split an order of magret de canard aux pêches & légumes de saison (duck breast with peaches & seasonal vegetables).

"This is fabulous," Antoinette said. "I guess the meal doesn't have to be entirely soufflés."

Manon nodded happily with her mouth full.

Dessert was not to be omitted.

"Should we each order something and then switch dishes halfway through eating them?" Antonette asked.

Manon's eyes lit up like this was the best idea.

"Oui, oui, s'il vous plaît!" she said.

After another quick perusal of the menu, they chose the soufflé framboise & compotée de rhubarbe (raspberry souffle & rhubarb compote) and the soufflé pistache & sauce chocolat (pistachio souffle & chocolate sauce).

When the waiter brought the desserts, he carefully placed them in front of Antoinette and Manon. They were perfectly formed and smelled very enticing. Then he held a plain white sauce boats directly over the small holes in the center and poured the sauces in with a flourish.

The souffles were things of beauty, and they tasted even better: hot, but not scalding, with the most delectable blend of chocolate infused in one, and rhubarb sauce in the other.

"If this isn't gastronomic heaven, I don't know what is," Antoinette said, enjoying every bite.

Manon agreed. "Totally worth it!"

When they had eaten all of that and paid their bill, the dolls left to take a walk in the sunshine through the Jardin des Tuileries.

Its name refers to the kilns for tiles that once occupied that spot. The garden was created after the kilns had been removed.

At the eastern end of it was the Arc de Triomphe du Carrousel built by Napoleon to celebrate his victories. The Louvre was just beyond it.

Expanses of uniformly green lawns surrounded by gorgeous and meticulously tended shrubs and flower beds stretched from one end of the gardens to the other. Irises of every color graced them.

A large round pool of water, called the Grand Bassin Rond (ground round basin) was in the center, with other, small basins nearby.

The dolls wandered happily around the gardens, admiring them, until they had seen everything. Another large basin, the Bassin Octagonal, was at the western end of the garden.

Near it, they noticed a small ice cream shop, and planned to return another day with their fiancés.

It had been a wonderful afternoon.

Le Palais Garnier – The Paris Opera House

It should come as no surprise that the Paris Opera House wasn't called that by the French.

The Parisians called it Le Palais Garnier, and it certainly was a palace to music. Named for its architect, Jean-Louis Garnier, it was a beautiful structure, inside and out, and its dome was adorned with ceiling murals by the artist Marc Chagall.

Antoinette was looking forward to seeing the performers of the Paris Opéra and performing with them again. She always enjoyed that.

She had arranged a matinée concert that matches its venue: she would not only play the violin, but would also sing selections from *The Phantom of the Opera.*

Antoinette will sing as Christine Daaé, the heroine of that story, including "Think of Me," "I Remember," "All I Ask of You," "Wishing You Were Somehow Here Again," and, of course, "The Phantom of the Opera."

But that wasn't all; she wouldn't be doing just one concert on this trip.

Antoinette will play with the Paris Opéra as it performed a ballet: *Le Parc* by Angelin Preljocaj. It is an interesting one; Mozart concertos and sonatas were blended with modern music to create a dreamlike atmosphere for contemporary and classical dance. It is set in a stylized 18th century garden, and follows a pair of lovers from timid encounters to intense, sensual abandon.

She will be there for a week as a guest, to play her Stradivarius violin with the orchestra for several of the ballet's performances.

She hadn't spent this much time in Paris for a while, so Antoinette was very happy to be doing this. She loved the music, and enjoyed the adventurous mixture of Mozart's work with modern tunes.

Ileandra was in Mumbai, India, at Jasvinder's house, and wearing a sari that suited her almost-ghostly pale complexion.

Jasvinder had selected it from her closet taking that into consideration along with the alien's difficulty coping with extreme heat. "You should be okay wearing this," she told her.

Jasvinder was wearing a lavender-periwinkle-purple-on-white sari with a gorgeous lotus pattern. "It's our national flower," she told Ileandra.

The alien was fascinated to hear that. "Humans have national flowers for each of their nations?"

"Yes, we do. Let's get you into this sari."

They had fun getting Ileandra dressed in it.

"This is a choli," Jasvinder had said, holding up a white, close-fitting, short-sleeved shirt. That wasn't at all difficult to put on.

Next, Jasvinder held out a skirt, saying "This is a ghagra." It had pockets. "I'm like Antoinette that way," she said. "I always want pockets. Pickpockets can't get at my keys and wallet."

Last came the sari – the part of the outfit that the entire ensemble went by. Jasvinder folded the pretty, block-printed long rectangle lengthwise in half, then folded each side back upon itself.

"Hold still," she said to Ileandra. "I'm going to pin one end to your left shoulder." She did this with a safety pin, leaving a length of the sari to hang down the back. "That part is called a pallu," she said.

Ileandra was having a great time with this. "I wouldn't be able to put this beautiful outfit on without you," she said, "and the thin cotton is so comfortable!"

Jasvinder smiled as she wound the sari around and around the alien. Fold, tuck, fold, tuck, fold, tuck…and everything was in place.

"You look good!" Jasvinder said approvingly. "That should help you cope with the heat here." She also gave the alien a parasol to use.

Mumbai is on the west coast of India, in the state of Maharashtra, facing the Arabian Sea. Its name derives from the goddess Mumbadevi of the native Koli community, and it means "mother" in the Maharathi language.

The city is home to Bollywood, India's film industry, where Jasvinder worked as a sitar player and sometimes as an actress, still playing her sitar.

Mumbai consists of seven islands. The smaller ones are called, in order from south to north, Colaba, Old Woman's Island (also known as Little Colaba), the Isle of Bombay, Mazagaon, Parel, Worli, and Mahim.

There are also several smaller islands, and north of them all is the much larger Sashti Island, also known as Salsette Island. Mumbai includes the southern part of it.

Jasvinder lived in a historic district with her parents and sister. Her fiancé lived nearby. The house was in the historic district of Bandra West. It was a beautiful old bungalow, made of wood with intricately shaped, blue-painted arches and eaves, on a brick-paved street with similar houses.

Ileandra had arrived the night before.

To get there, the alien had had her ship go to a spot outside the city, to the north, in Sanjay Gandhi National Park. The area offered plenty of tree cover for the ship to hover low to the ground where it wouldn't be seen from a distance.

Jasvinder and her fiancé had driven to a spot past the butterfly garden, down the path, and around the bend. Then they had pulled over and waited.

Almost immediately, a ship appeared to their left. The cloaking device had been disengaged. There was a flash of light, and then Ileandra appeared below it. Then the ship waited a moment, seeming to watch.

Jasvinder and her fiancé had immediately gotten out of the car and waved. Ileandra walked over to them and Jasvinder gave her a hug in greeting as her awestruck fiancé watched. The alien hugged her back, and turned to shake hands with him.

Then they looked back at the ship.

"My boyfriend is watching to make sure that I really get picked up before he lets the ship leave," Ileandra told them.

As if on cue, the cloaking device abruptly came back on, disappearing the ship.

"Wow…" the two humans said.

Ileandra smiled. "It does look pretty amazing when I know that I'm safely with friends and can go back to my ship later," she said.

They looked at her, taking that in, and then ushered her into the car. All she had with her was her gray kit bag. She was wearing her work clothing again – a blue outfit of a shirt and long pants with pockets.

Jasvinder's fiancé drove them back to her family's house, where she met her sister and parents. Everyone was amazed to meet a real alien and hear about her work as a botanist.

After plying Ileandra with hot, soft, fresh vegetable chaat and samosas, the fiancé left and the family showed her to her room. Jasvinder stuck around for a while, chatting with Ileandra about what they would do during her visit.

"How long are you here for?" she asked.

"A week. Antoinette has gone to play with the Royal Hawaiian Band in Hawaii, and taken Manon with her to see the museums. Their fiancés are taking care of their cats, so I'm off on my own. Is that amount of time okay? If not, I can call my ship earlier."

"Of course it's okay! This is terrific! I am going to show you the spice markets and stock you up with lots of fragrant, fresh, perfect spices and hot peppers. We'll get you a mango tree, too."

The alien botanist was delighted. "Oh…thank you so much! I'm going to love this visit. And I'm so lucky to have you for a host. Are you sure that you won't miss any work while I'm here?"

"Don't worry; I practice my sitar each morning, and again later in the afternoon. I have one gig at Film City – that's it. It's in the middle of the week, so you can rest here while I'm gone. We should have lots of time to shop for spices."

And they did.

The next morning, Jasvinder's mother made chai tea and breakfast for everyone. Ileandra watched her make the chai. It included a cup of hot water for each person, another cup of milk for each, cardamom pods, sugar, and fresh slices of ginger.

The chai was just part of the breakfast, which included a sweet mango lassi, granola, and fresh parathas, which were round, warm flatbreads.

Jasvinder's father left for the financial district of the city, her sister went to see a friend, and then her mother did yoga with them before Jasvinder practiced her sitar for a few hours.

Before they left, Jasvinder found the alien studying some figurines in the living room. One of them was a beautiful woman with eight arms. The other was an anthropomorphized elephant with four arms, sitting in the lotus position.

"That's Durga, the Hindu goddess of protection, strength, motherhood, and wars. And dharma, which means peace and cosmic order. The other one is Ganesh. The god of destruction, Shiva, considered him to be too alluring, so he replaced Ganesh's head with that of an elephant."

The alien stared at her and the statue. She would read up on Hinduism later, she decided, when Jasvinder was busy practicing her sitar.

In the afternoon, before lunch, they got into Jasvinder's car and drove to the Mirchi Galli spice market in Lalbaug. They parked and walked in the direction that Jasvinder was leading. The scents of the spices wafted in the air all around them so intensely that Ileandra could smell them before they even saw the place.

They stepped into the shop, which was open to the air at the front, and a burst of bright color was revealed to go along with the spices. "This is so different from the spice section of an American grocery store," Ileandra commented.

Jasvinder grinned. Then she gave the alien a tour of everything, ordering some of each to be packed as she did so: saffron, cardamom, vanilla beans, nutmeg, cloves, cinnamon, star anise, and turmeric. She showed Ileandra the peppers; there were so many colors of them, both fresh and dried!

Soon, Jasvinder's shopping bag was full of some of what seemed to be everything in the shop.

They thanked the shop owner and stepped back out onto the street. Jasvinder had also bought coconuts, cashews, and almonds. Ileandra had tiny teeth, but she bravely tried an almond, whole, for her first time. It was delicious.

She looked around. There were lots of other spice shops on the street, plus some that sold paper lanterns. A large statue of Ganesh guarded a beautiful tower of a small temple. Men on motorcycles and women in saris were out and about.

Jasvinder led the way to another shop that sold different types of lentils: red, yellow, and brown. "We use them to make dal, a staple that is sort of a soup and sort of a sauce," she told the alien.

At yet another shop they found asafoetida. This spice was sold raw in a jar. "The smell would bother people if it weren't in the jar," Jasvinder explained. "We use it in dal. It is sprinkled over the pot to temper the spices, which include turmeric."

From there, they found some street food for lunch. Jasvinder bought two of what resembled vegan burgers with a spicy vegetable curry over a baked potato sliced in half between the pieces of bread. "This is called pav bhaji," she said.

At another nearby stall, she bought them cups of chaas to drink. This was a sweet buttermilk drink flavored with spices that had been roasted before being stirred in: cumin and mustard seeds, curry leaves, asafoetida, grated ginger, and finely diced green chiles. It was good.

They enjoyed the food as they walked along, perusing the stalls some more.

Each day of the week except for one, when Jasvinder had a gig to play for a movie, they went out in the afternoon and did something.

Another day, they had fig juice with dahi puri, a street food that looked like a pouch of bread broken open at the top and stuffed with chickpeas, covered with beaten yogurt, sprinkled with sev (dried chickpea noodles) and green mung beans, and garnished with juicy red pomegranate seeds.

In the middle of the week, Jasvinder took her friend to the Chhatrapati Shivaji Maharaj Vastu Sangrahalaya. It was a museum dedicated to the history of Mumbai from prehistoric to modern times. They enjoyed their afternoon there.

At the end of the week, Jasvinder drove them to the Mahindra Nursery. They asked to see the mango trees. After choosing a Bombay variety tree and having it set aside, they continued to look around.

"I have to consider how much room my car has to transport all these trees," Jasvinder said. "Of course, I'm out without my sitar, so that helps," she added with a laugh.

A pomegranate tree was added to their order.

There were several Ayurvedic medicinal plants for sale, and Ileandra chose one of each. Soon the back seat was full, but Jasvinder wasn't concerned.

"My fiancé won't let us go to the park without him at night," she said, "but we can put a few of these potted plants on the empty seat and floor around our legs if necessary."

That evening, it was time for Ileandra to go back to her ship. Jasvinder's fiancé arrived for dinner, which was another spice-infused delight. The alien now knew about eating from a thali, and had amused and surprised her host's family when she complimented it, saying, "The left side of the thali is arranged so beautifully!"

Jasvinder's mother looked pleased, but a bit puzzled until she told her mother, "Ileandra has been spending lots of time online reading whatever she could find about our culture, particularly the cuisine and how to appreciate it."

Everyone laughed. "It worked," Jasvinder's father told the alien, who grinned back.

When the meal was over, it was time to pack the car. Ileandra was dressed in her blue pants and shirt again, and carrying her gray kit bag.

After loading the trunk with all that it could hold, the trees and potted plants were strategically placed around the cabin of the car. It just fit.

They drove off, and Ileandra signaled her ship to meet her where they had gone a week earlier.

Again, in the darkness, the hovering, round craft appeared, casting an eerie but sufficient light over the ground near the car.

With a flash, Jasvinder's boyfriend beamed down.

He was dressed as she was, and had short blond hair and huge, almond-shaped blue eyes. Like hers, his mouth and nose were smaller than a human's.

"Namaste," he said to Jasvinder and her fiancé.

They smiled, pleased with the greeting, and said, "Namaste" back to him with their hands steepled. They also bowed to him.

He did the same.

Ileandra was smiling.

A moment later, everyone went to work taking all of the spices, nuts, herbs, lentils, chiles, and plants out of the car. Everything was placed directly under the ship, where the alien's boyfriend had appeared.

Another flash, and the lot of it was gone.

"Wow," said Jasvinder's fiancé. "That made short work of everything."

"It will be a bit more work once we join it," the alien boyfriend said, grinning.

"Thank you very, very much for everything," Ileandra said. "It was a wonderful, fascinating, delicious, delectable week and I enjoyed every bit of it," she told the humans, hugging Jasvinder.

"It was my pleasure," Jasvinder replied, hugging her back.

She and her fiancé stood by the car and watched as the two aliens stood under their ship and vanished in one last flash of light.

Then they got back into their car and drove away.

It was a rainy day; perfect for a fundraiser.

Antoinette was going to the now defunded local Public Broadcasting Service station to participate in one. She remembered the word she used as a teenager for this: beg-a-thon. It fit.

She was about to record a message in which she would plead for viewers to donate money to keep PBS going, and NPR – National Public Radio.

Book banning would be discussed, too.

All of the dolls were wearing dresses with fabric patterns that depicted books. Antoinette's, Manon's, and Lilith's dresses had books with no titles. Their books could have been about anything.

But Mallory's dress was clearly all about potion making. It didn't get much more witchy than that.

"I figured that if we're going to bash the idiocy of book banning, I might as well wear something that would actually be a target of that," she said.

The others laughed, pleased with that.

Antoinette thought of why they were doing this. "Damn Herr Pumpkingropenfuhrer," she said as they arrived at the WNET-TV Channel 13 building in Manhattan. "He tanks everything he touches financially. Ruining entertainment with fascism will do this. He ordered that the algorithms that AI uses incorporate his world view, with fascism, be added to education, news, and entertainment. That will stultify creativity and poison freedom of speech."

"Yeah," Lilith said. "Tell us something we don't know." She was carrying a cake that Antoinette had baked for the staff. It depicted the Cookie Monster character from *Sesame Street*. She wasn't actually tired of hearing this, though, or she wouldn't be there.

Mallory asked, "What kind of cake did you make? The frosting is perfect for this occasion, but what's under it?" She was grinning as she peeked into the box while they rode the elevator.

"Lavender cream cake with chocolate frosting," Antoinette replied. "Except for the decoration — that's tinted white chocolate with a few bittersweet chocolate chips."

They walked up to the front desk, and the director came over to meet them.

Antoinette thanked the director for having her there, introduced her friends, and opened the box to reveal the cake.

The director's eyes popped, and she immediately said she wanted it shown on their broadcast.

Lilith and Mallory grinned from ear-to-ear; this was going to be a fun event.

"Shall we talk about the fact that Herr Pumpkingropenfuhrer wants the American voting public to be kept ignorant and therefore easy to manipulate? Tell them that our democracy depends upon keeping public broadcasting funded, and that book banning must stop?"

"I'm counting on you to say all that – on live television – repeatedly."

The witches grinned some more.

Antoinette grinned too, and said, "I will!"

Manon was right them. Her beautiful, books-themed dress showed some plants and vases. She greeted the director cheerfully. "I came to help you with the event. I even brought some books that were banned hundreds of years ago."

It was a book that the Puritans had banned in 1637 for criticizing their religion. It was Thomas Morton's *New English Canaan.*

Everyone stared at it, intrigued.

"It's always the religious members of any society who start this nonsense. They don't want a separation of religion and state," Lilith commented.

That wasn't all.

Manon had Harriet Beecher Stowe's *Uncle Tom's Cabin*, Mark Twain's *The Adventures of Huckleberry Finn*, Salman Rushdie's *The Satanic Verses*, and two Shakespeare plays: *Twelfth Night*, which depicted gender fluidity, and *MacBeth*, which had been banned for showing witches.

"'Bubble, bubble, toil and trouble,'" Mallory said, picking it up with a smile.

The director was absolutely delighted, and had a table placed in front of the camera for the books.

"Speaking of witches and fascism," Antoinette said in a low tone, pulling Lilith off to the side of the room, "I'm really worried that Manon is here. If she is seen on television, photographed, written about, and ICE discovers that she is not yet a U.S. citizen but has the audacity to criticize fascism in the United States, she could get grabbed at any time."

Lilith listened, then said, "Don't worry. I have my hand on my wand, and I'm charming and spelling her way through this event. I'll tell her to lay low, but they won't get her."

Antoinette breathed a big sigh of relief.

"Thank you," she said.

Lilith smiled. "She's my friend, too. And no one deserves what ICE and the Orange Moron's gang of thugs are perpetrating."

Antoinette nodded and they rejoined the group.

It turned out to be a very productive afternoon.

They went live with their presentation, which was recorded. It would be used over and over again, every time one of Antoinette's concerts was broadcast. The PBS station had plenty of recorded concerts from the Metropolitan Opera to use.

The cake was a hit, too, as the director emphasized the necessity of continuing children's literacy programs, and the diversity, equality, and inclusiveness that Sesame Street was famous for.

Julia, the autistic Muppet, presented the cake.

Antoinette was thrilled to meet her.

"That was terrific!" Mallory said as they got out of the elevator and stepped into the lobby.

Anntoinette nodded. "I wish I could do more than this," she said as the group walked out of the TV station.

Lilith and Mallory exchanged looks…and grins.

Antoinette must have more plans, they seemed to be thinking.

Mallory went back to work after the PBS event with Antoinette, Lilith, and Manon.

She was on rounds, checking in with her patients, when her phone rang. (Well…it "hooted." She had its ringtone set to make quiet owl sounds.)

Checking the number, she saw that it was a call routed from the Silphium Society hotline. 'Uh-oh, she thought. 'I'm on duty. I can't leave.'

Nevertheless, she felt duty-bound to at least answer and find out what was going on. Maybe she didn't need to go anywhere…

"Hello?" she said. "I'm a gynecologist. How can I help you?" She was supposed to be anonymous, for security reasons, so she withheld her name.

A stressed-out woman was on the other end. "I'm pregnant, I live with my boyfriend, and I want to keep it. But we live in Tennessee. My doctor is refusing to treat me because he doesn't approve of the fact that my boyfriend and I aren't married, yet I am pregnant."

Mallory swore under her breath.

Then she said, "Let me guess," as she headed for her office. "He's religious, and the newly minted Medical Ethics Defense Act in your state allows him to abrogate his duties as a physician, so he's inflicting his judgment of your choices on you."

"Yes, he is. And he's putting that ahead of me."

"Religion is culture. Religiousness is poison," Mallory said into her phone. "I say that a lot."

She didn't wait for a response; she just kept moving down the hall until she arrived at her office.

"Okay. I was walking to my office once I answered my phone and found out what this is about. I'm at work, on rounds."

"Oh! I hope I'm not keeping you from your patients!" the woman on the phone said, sounding apologetic.

"No! Not at all. I've just checked them all, as a matter of fact." Mallory settled into her seat in front of her computer and called up some websites.

"So…obviously you need to fire that poor excuse for a physician. What is he, by the way?" A general practitioner, a gynecologist, what?"

"He's a GP. We live in a rural area."

"I see. Can you tell me exactly where, so I can look up the closest alternatives to where you live? I want to find you a replacement who lives within a realistic driving distance for you to manage."

The woman told her that she lived in eastern Tennessee.

"Okay. That's a start. I'll need to look around on the internet, so if I'm not very talkative for a minute here and there, that's why."

"Okay…thank you!"

"You're welcome," Mallory said, and set about searching for someone else to treat this patient. 'If I can find a woman doctor for her, perhaps someone I know, I will,' she thought to herself.

Her next thought was an angry, oft-repeated one: 'The nerve of men to think for a nanosecond that they ought to have the slightest say over women's choices and lives and health!'

Aloud, she chatted amiably and, she hoped, soothingly with her patient as she searched. Fortunately, this woman lived near her state's border with Virginia. Abortion in that state was legal through the second trimester of pregnancy. Perhaps she could find a doctor in that state…

"There!" Mallory suddenly said. "I found a woman gynecologist about an hour from you in Virginia. Can you use her services with your healthcare?"

The woman on the other end of the call said, "Tell me her information and we'll look it up. My boyfriend is sitting at the computer here with me, and he has our provider information ready to compare it with."

'Good,' Mallory thought. 'At least this patient seems to be in a safe relationship, just from what I can tell from this phone call.' She told the woman the name, phone number, and address of the gynecologist she had found.

There was a pause during which Mallory could here keys on a computer keyboard clicking.

Then she heard, "Yes! We can see her. Thank you very much! I probably could have found her myself, but we panicked."

"That's perfectly natural, and okay! I'm glad I could help. Call her and see if you can get an appointment. If you have any trouble, call back and I'll look for another doctor. If I don't hear from you, I'll know you are connected with a good replacement doctor."

Sighs of relief were let out on the other end.

"Thank you so much!" the woman said. "I'll do that…or not, if this goes as we hope."

With that, they ended the call.

Mallory hoped for the best, and waited to hear from that woman again, but she never did.

She was glad.

And she just knew, without knowing every little detail of every woman in anti-choice, religious nationalist states, that many more women were having the same issue.

Holiday in a Divided Nation

Antoinette had some strange thoughts as she made her annual 4th of July dessert, a raspberry-blueberry tart with Neufchâtel cheese whipped with honey, confectioner's sugar, and vanilla.

"Democrats and Republicans…" she muttered to herself, looking at the colors of the fruit. "I'm a political liberal, yet red raspberries are my favorite fruit. Taste buds don't care about politics."

She made a glaze of raspberry preserves heated and whisked with rosewater.

Her fiancé looked up at her from his phone.

"Ridiculous!" she said in a louder tone, still looking at the tart. "They're just red and blue berries, for the 4th of July. These colors belong to everyone."

"So much for 'As American as apple pie,' then," he remarked.

"I love raspberries more than apple pie, which lacks the colors of our flag anyway," she replied.

They grinned at the logic of that.

"I'm going to sing our national anthem for a divided nation, one that should keep religion and state separate, but try to ignore all that today and just appreciate our lives in our home country."

She would be singing at the National Mall; they were at her Washington, D.C. apartment for the holiday. Her parents were home in Connecticut. They would watch *A Capitol Fourth* on PBS, which still had money to function, and see her sing.

Maybe after the Oval Office was rid of its orange occupant she would feel better about this.

Meanwhile, Herr Pumpkingropenfuhrer had fired the board of trustees of the John F. Kennedy Center for the Performing Arts in Washington, D.C. and appointed someone from his staff to run it.

He did this to prevent free artistic expression and liberal views from being expressed in its performances. Therefore, Antoinette would boycott that concert venue until he was out of office. She was not alone in this.

The Pumpkingropenfuhrer had also said that he was planning to rename the venue after himself.

'That really is going too far,' she thought.

The name of a past president should not be erased. This fiend was already busily erasing Kennedy's legacy, having dismantled U.S. AID and the Peace Corps. He was an international as well as national disgrace and embarrassment.

Antoinette was having a lot of trouble feeling a sense of national pride on her nation's birthday, but she went to the National Mall anyway.

When the time came, she sang beautifully, forgetting what was wrong with the world long enough to give a lively performance that everyone enjoyed and appreciated.

But…the joy evaporated quickly.

As she was walking away to rejoin her fiancé, some men in plain suits approached her.

One of them was carrying an envelope.

Antoinette grimly thought to herself, 'Am I about to be served with some horrid legal papers?!'

But she let them talk to her.

There were two of them.

The one with the envelope held it out to her, while the other said, "President #$%@ would like you to perform for him at the White House. He asks that you sing Laura Branigan's song, "Gloria," and play a medley on your violin of themes from the Village People."

Antoinette was outraged.

One reason was that the Village People were a band that could perform their own work. They could sue her if she did that.

She pointed this out to the men.

They glanced at each other, nonplussed.

It came as no surprise to her that they hadn't thought this part of the request through and had simply gone to do the orange moron's bidding.

The other reason for Antoinette's rage needed no further explanation here; by now, the reader knows all about it.

Without further ado she said, "Tell him that I will never perform anything for him. I don't want to."

"You don't want to perform for the president of the United States?" asked the other of the two.

"No. I don't. Not this undemocratic, fascist misogynist. I will not do anything for him but wait for his term to end. I don't want him."

"But you just performed here…"

"I performed here because this place belongs to all Americans. It is not affiliated with either political party. Here we are on the steps of a monument dedicated to a president who ended slavery. Anyone ought to be proud of that legacy."

They stared at her, nonplussed.

"Happy 4th of July," she said to them.

They said it back and left.

She had not been able to say "Happy Independence Day" this year. She just didn't feel the same safety and sense of independence that she had felt in the past anymore…not even when past presidents from the other political party had been in office. This was just different.

When she and her fiancé met up and left to return home for the evening, she told him what the men had said; he had seen them talking.

He hoped that she wouldn't have any trouble traveling internationally because of this.

"Fortunately, I have dual French and American citizenship. I don't usually do anything much with it, but if I need to, I will. I won't let Herr Pumpkingropenfuhrer hold anything over me."

And she wouldn't let him discover what else she was up to as she resisted him, either.

She looked forward to going home to Connecticut, away from this marble city, and away from intrusive requests.

She never wanted to be in the presence of that evil, self-absorbed threat to democracy and offense to humanity.

It was consistently both American and French to reject any semblance of having a king, which is what Herr Pumpkingropenfuhrer wanted to be.

Never!

Willow Fears Border Crossings

Willow was visiting Manon and her cat, Dauphine, who was napping on a chair.

She was there to ask Manon to feed her own cat, Eleanore.

"Of course!" Manon said without a moment's hesitation. "You can bring her over the day before you leave, with whatever food you want me to give her, and her bed and toys."

"Merci beaucoup!" Willow said, smiling.
"De rien," Manon replied, laying out a beautiful gingerbread cheesecake with cinnamon cream that she had made for their visit, and pouring lattes.

The doorbell to Manon's apartment rang.
It was Mallory.

Manon let her in, and then turned to Willow to say, "I told her that you were anxious about your trip home to see your parents, and I can relate. My fiancé wants us to get married as soon as possible, so that we won't have to worry about that. It's already an ordeal to go to work in Paris and back here, and I haven't dared go to see my parents when they're in Belgium, because that's not work-related."

Mallory had come to say that she would travel in and out of Canada with Willow because she was going at the same time to speak at a medical conference.

"Your American husband will be with you, too," Mallory reminded her. "That should help a lot. But I will make sure that you get through when you come back." She grinned, showing them her wand.

Willow breathed a sigh of relief.

Manon poured Mallory a latte, and they sat comfortably enjoying the cheesecake and chatting about the details of the upcoming trip.

Dauphine watched them calmly, with a cat smile.

Willow wondered, however, how she and Eleanore would get along.

"Oh, don't worry," Manon said. "We take care of my fiancé's sister's cat whenever she travels out of state. Her cat is female, too, and they get along well. Just make sure to bring Eleanore's bed and toys."

Willow smiled, reassured, and said she would.

Emergency at Sea

The *Yemoja* was anchored for the night off of the Cayman Islands. It was beautiful out: perfectly clear, with a view of the stars that would delight an astronomer.

But that wasn't the branch of science that Nichelle was here for. She had had a leisurely afternoon of snorkeling. She even met a stingray.

It had gone right past her, uninterested in her.

She did get a good look at it, though. She saw its eyes casually look her over as it passed her, spiracles breathing just behind each one.

Then it was gone.

She saw lots of lionfish, a beautiful but invasive species with long red-and-white stripes all over its body and fins.

Nichelle enjoyed her drama-free time in the water, and came back aboard the boat after gathering samples of water, sand, and plastic debris.

Early in the day, the three female students, Shondra, Jeanne, and Leah, had taken their passports, climbed into the dinghy, and gone ashore with shopping bags to resupply the galley with fresh fish. At least, that was their stated purpose.

Nichelle wasn't fooled. They wanted to explore the island for the afternoon, and she had let them go. Why not?

The men, Diego and Andreas, had wasted their breath pointing out that there were plenty of fish in the sea.

Nichelle had laughed. "You can stay here then, and miss out on a perk of this summer internship: tourism."

The chagrined looks on their faces were amusing.

Too late – the dinghy was gone, and they had to mind the boat while their professor snorkeled!

Hours later, the women returned with their bags full of fish, including snapper and lionfish. The George Town Waterfront sold what was caught early in the day.

Nichelle wanted to hear about their excursion, so they told her that they had eaten lunch at Morgan's Seafood Restaurant.

"Oh, that's a great restaurant! What did you eat?"

Jeanne said, "I had the catch of the day, which was lionfish. It came with a lemon ginger butter sauce and basmati rice. It was really good, so we bought some later at the fish market."

Shondra and Leah had tried the seafood crepes.

"What was in those?" Nichelle asked. "I forgot."

"Shrimp, scallops, and fish – snapper, they told us," Shondra answered.

"It was delicious," Leah added.

"We also tried the fresh catch ceviche," Shondra said. "It was beautiful, with fresh flower petals."

"Interesting…" Nichelle said. "They must have changed their presentation a bit since I was last there, to keep current with restaurant trends."

The men looked really sorry they had missed it.

They also seemed to be taking notes on what impressed the women, who found this entertaining, though they made no comment about that.

Jeannc showed the fish that they had bought at the George Town Waterfront fish market. "We bought snapper, lionfish – we ought to eat sustainably – salmon, tuna, and this really long wahoo," she concluded.

There were also six lobsters, which elicited cheers all around.

Leah took the wahoo to the galley right away; it was quite long. Wahoo were long, silvery game fish with long, pointed mouths.

Jeanne was looking forward to using a cookbook she had brought, *The Complete Cayman Island Cookbook: Authentic and Simple Cayman Island Recipes From Sunrise to Sunset*. She had read the recipes before embarking on the trip, and supplied the galley with the necessary spices to try some of the recipes in it.

"What else did you do and see?" Nichelle asked.

Uncertain glances were exchanged among the women. Leah had come back on deck in time to hear this question.

"Come on, I expected you to take advantage of the chance to travel on land during this trip!" Nichelle said, grinning.

The three of them breathed a sigh of relief and grinned back.

"We bought the fish right after lunch, so we wouldn't miss out," Leah said first.

Nichelle rolled her eyes. "I could see that."

"We wandered around to look at the souvenirs and jewelry," Shondra said.

Each of them had bought necklaces and earrings with brightly colored, large beads in hues of blue and greens.

"Now we know where yours must have come from," Leah said.

"Yes – you've seen me wear them to teach class."

Jeanne was in a hurry to go down to the galley and start cooking the lobsters. She was going to make a coconut sauce for them, and little rum cakes with her mini bundt pan. It had six wells in it.

"You do realize that you're not on this trip to do gourmet cooking, right?" Andreas teased.

She stuck her tongue out at him and measured out the cake ingredients.

Nichelle laughed.

She turned around to help put the rest of the fish away, some in the freezer and some in the fridge.

Leah had cut the wahoo into sections and put one in the fridge. Its head stared out at her from the middle shelf. Nichelle put a salmon and a lionfish next to it and shut the door.

She turned around to see Shondra at the counter, setting up salad ingredients. Something about her worried Nichelle, but after a moment, Shondra seemed fine.

Dinner was a well-appreciated feast.

So was dessert; Jeanne's run bundt cakelets were a success. "Don't expect me to do this often, though," she warned with a grin. "We're supposed to be studying!"

Everyone laughed.

Shondra looked preoccupied and anxious, but she laughed along with the rest of the group.

The next day, though, Shondra declined to go out snorkeling, saying that she had her period.

Nichelle suspected that it was more than that, but didn't pry. She wouldn't, unless and/or until she believed that Shondra had more than that going on.

By the middle of the next day, however, Shondra was staying on her bunk, staring up at the bunk above, eyes blank. Her arms were tight around her.

Nichelle went and looked at her.

"Shondra?" she said, and touched her face.

She was burning up.

"What's going on, Shondra?" she asked.

"I don't know," Shondra said, sounding scared. "I took RU486. I got it on the island. I had it sent to me. I took it exactly as directed, at the right times, spaced apart, and did everything correctly. I'm sure of it. But I don't feel the way it said I would."

"How do you feel?"

"Like something's wrong. The blood doesn't smell right. I passed something small – I only missed one period, so that didn't surprise me – and the bleeding is still going on, but there's also a discharge of something else with it."

"Show me," Nichelle said.

"It's in the bathroom garbage; on top, folded over," Shondra told her.

Nichelle checked; a soaked maxi pad was there. She took it to the sink, unfolded it, pulled the wings open, and looked. Pus and blood. There should have only been blood there.

'Damn…' Nichelle thought. She took out her phone and called the Silphium Society hotline.

It was late afternoon.

Leah came in as Mallory answered the phone.

"Shondra? Can I get you anything?"

Shondra just shook her head.

Leah touched her and said, "You're on fire!"

Meanwhile, Nichelle was talking to Mallory, explaining the situation.

"Tell me your coordinates," Mallory said.

Nichelle had to go up on deck to do that, but she soon had them. The boat was moving toward Jamaica at this point.

Mallory asked her to stop the boat, drop the anchor, and wait for her to get there.

They ended the call, and Nichelle ordered Andreas to stop the boat and lower the anchor.

"What's going on?" he asked.

"We're having an emergency at sea," she told him. "And we're staying at sea for it. Help is on the way."

"Should I call anyone?"

"No. I already did that."

"Oh. Okay."

Nichelle hoped he would take that at face value and not summon a coast guard or anything else. Mallory would be enough once she arrived.

She went back down to the bunk beds and found Jeanne and Leah with Shondra. They were putting cool washcloths on her face and arms and talking to her in low tones.

Good. At least no one was going to upset her.

'Thanks, Louisiana and other nearby states, for blocking abortion care,' Nichelle thought angrily.

Mallory to the rescue.

She was on her way, and had been at the hospital when she took Nichelle's call. She had stuffed her medical bag with antibiotics and fresh syringes on her way out, rushed home to get her broomstick, and taken off as fast as she could.

It was still light out as she took off, so she cast a spell to avoid being noticed by anyone as she flew.

Keeping low to the ground and diving into tree-covered areas part of the time, Mallory flew south. It took her an hour to get to the Gulf of Mexico.

From there, it was another quarter hour before she got to the Yemoja.

She landed on the deck, hopped off her broomstick, and only spared a glance at Andreas and Diego to ask where the patient was.

They stared back in shock, speechless.

"Take me to the patient NOW," she said sternly. "You can be amazed at the manner of my arrival later. This is a medical emergency, and I'm a physician. The witch part of me is another story, for another time."

The guys seemed to snap out of it.

"She's downstairs, straight ahead, and back to the left," Andreas told her.

"Thank you," Mallory said, and rushed down there.

"Hi Nichelle!" she said, arriving at Shondra's bunk bed.

"Hi. Thank you for coming," Nichelle said.

"It's what I do," Mallory said, turning immediately to Shondra. "So…your name is Shondra," she said with a businesslike smile. "Your professor told me that. I'm Dr. Mallory Moonmist. I'm a gynecologist. I work in New York City."

Shondra, Jeanne, and Leah all stared at her.

"And you just happened to be in the Caribbean Sea?" Leah asked, incredulous.

Mallory smiled. "No, I didn't. We'll talk about that later. Shondra needs some help urgently."

Leah and Jeanne were willing to put their questions about Mallory on hold. They hovered nearby in case she needed them to get anything.

Mallory had put her medical bag on the table next to Shondra's bunk. It normally served as a desk. Nichelle closed the laptop and moved everything off to one side.

Mallory examined Shondra, asked her lots of questions, and stood up. "You have a fever because not all of the tissue was expelled from your body," she said.

"My boyfriend and I used a condom, but I don't think it worked," Shondra said.

Mallory replied, "They're not 100 percent effective, but that's what mifepristone is for. Let me take a look at the pads you've used already."

Nichelle showed them to her.

"Can you get it out of me, or have I ruined the summer research trip?" Shondra asked, looking apologetically at her professor.

"Don't worry about the research trip!" Nichelle said. "Let's just make sure you're okay. None of this is your fault. It's just bad luck."

Mallory smiled at her, then looked serious again.

"You should be okay, but I will have to work quickly. Please get up and pee first; I'm going to try to get it out of you by pushing and manipulating your uterus while you lie still, and you need to be empty when I do that."

Leah and Jeanne helped Shondra get up. She was shaky and dizzy. They walked her over to the head to use the toilet, steadying her as she stood up to wash her hands.

Nichelle glanced back at the galley and the stairway. Diego and Andreas had crept down to see what was happening. They weren't in the women's bunk area, but they were peering at the group.

"Don't come over here," Nichelle said.

"We won't," Diego said. "Did we hear that doctor say she is a gynecologist?"

"Yes, you did," Nichelle said. "She's what we need. You haven't called anyone else, have you?"

"No." Diego said.

"Good. Let the doctor work."

The men nodded and sat down in the galley.

Shondra was laid back out on her bunk, waiting.

The other women shielded her from the men's view while Mallory worked.

Nichelle knew that Shondra had a boyfriend, but he was back in Louisiana; he wasn't one of the students on the *Yemoja*.

After several minutes of manipulation, something came out onto the pad that Leah had slipped under Shondra. It was dark, and not very large.

"Success!" Mallory said. "That's what we were looking for. Looks like endometrial tissue, and maybe embryonic matter. A pregnancy, if you really were in fact pregnant after missing just one period, wouldn't be obvious in this. But since you retained some tissue and developed a fever, you might very well have been."

Leah and Jeanne started cleaning Shondra and changing her bed pad.

Mallory continued, "I'm going to inject you with a large dose of antibiotics and leave you with a round of antibiotic pills to follow that up with. That should clear up any infection."

With that, she prepared a syringe, disinfected the designated spot, and slowly injected the contents into Shondra's upper arm.

"You need to visit a physician when you get back to New Orleans. Do you have one there?"

"Yes," Shondra said. "I'm from there."

Mallory had settled onto the desk chair. "Is this doctor pro-choice, or untrustworthy?"

Shondra smiled. "She's safe. She told me about the Silphium Society hotline. She did that when we were outside her office, when we met for ice cream in a park."

Nichelle and Mallory were relieved to hear that.

"I think you're going to be okay now," Mallory said. "But I want you to call me at the hotline number again to tell me how you're doing, just to make sure. I'll be checking in with you for the next few days to see how you're doing, until you are back to normal. If that doesn't happen, we'll figure something else out, but I think you'll be well in another day or so."

Nichelle breathed a big sigh of relief.

So did everyone else.

They could even hear the men doing that!

"So," Leah said, changing the subject. "How did you get here so fast?"

"She flew in on a broomstick," Andreas said.

Diego was holding it, and showed it to the women.

Nichelle recognized that purple broomstick.

She took it and handed it to Mallory.

"Thank you," the doctor said. "So…yes, I'm also a witch. That helps me to get to patients quickly, and, if there are anti-abortion tattle-tales around us, to do something about evidence and information leaks. Do I need to do anything more than destroy evidence?" she asked, looking sternly at the group.

Smiles all around. Each person affirmed her or himself as being pro-choice.

"Excellent!" the witch said. She took out her wand and burned the tissue over the galley sink.

She turned to face them, and they all nodded in approval. A chorus of "Thank yous" was spoken.

Mallory nodded, then gathered her things.

She went up the stairway and onto the deck.

Nichelle and everyone except Shondra came up with her, and waved as she flew off into the night.

Antoinette was working a busy schedule.

Jasvinder was back for another concert, this time at the Sunken Garden in Farmington, Connecticut, which was part of the estate of the Hill-Stead Museum.

The Hill-Stead was the family home of architect Theodate Pope Riddle, who had lived there with her parents and husband. Pope survived the May 7, 1915 sinking of the RMS *Lusitania* before that. She designed the buildings for the Avon Old Farms and Westover schools in Connecticut.

All of the other dolls were visiting, and of course attending this concert. That was how it looked to

outsiders; the real reason why they had come was to
hold a meeting of the Silphium Society.

Nichelle's summer aboard the Yemoja had been a
success, and all of her graduate students were doing
well. They had grants to continue their studies, and
all were healthy and happy, in part thanks to Mallory
and the work of the Silphium Society.

Manon had toured the house of the Hill-Stead
Museum and met with its curators – but just for the
enjoyment of seeing it, as it is to remain intact for
the viewing public. That was a provision of Pope's
will in 1946.

Antoinette and Jasvinder were playing in the little
oval-shaped gazebo in the middle of the garden. It
was a concert of quiet music, meant to be listened to
by people who sat in the chairs they had brought, or
heard as they walked around the garden.

Music wasn't the only activity taking place, though; poetry readings from members of the Connecticut Poetry Society would be part of the festivities. This was an annual event for the Sunken Garden, one that was planned carefully.

Antoinette played "Spring" and "Autumn" from Antonio Vivaldi's *The Four Seasons*, and then listened while Jasvinder played Bhajan in Raga Bhairavi.

A bhajan is a devotional song with a religious theme or spiritual ideas, and it means "sharing," and a Bharavi is classical, seven-pitch scale.

The dolls enjoyed the day outside, listening to their friends' beautiful music and to the poetry readings that alternate with it.

Willow particularly enjoyed one by an elderly man who reminisced in his about the deliveries of bottled milk when he was a child.

The poet, as a little boy, would climb into bed with his mother for a few minutes before it was time to get up, and he could hear the clinking sound as the milkman set the metal crate down on the doorstep. Then they would get up, take in the milk, and open the paraffin top. His mother let him lick the cream off of it.

Later on, Antoinette played Wolfgang Amadeus Mozart's *Eine kleine Nachtmusik*, (Serenade No. 13 for strings in G major), K. 525, composed in 1787. It translates as "a little night music."

Jasvinder played "Evening Raga" by Ravi Shankar.

When the event was over, it was time to leave and for the dolls to go back to Antoinette's house in Avon for their Silphium Society meeting.

This was about a review of activities, an update from Willow on the fiscal soundness of the organization, and reports from Lilith and Mallory about the legal and medical activities conducted.

They ordered two large pizzas from Luna Pizza with eggplant, spinach, garlic, basil, and bacon, and there was plenty of Blue Moon beer with orange slices to go around.

It was deeply satisfying for all to hear how well everything was going.

News reports were not picking up on much of their work, which was as it should be.

"We are delivering reproductive healthcare to women in forced birther states undetected, helping women to continue living independent lives, with bodily autonomy, and able to work and be happy," Mallory said with a smile.

Antoinette was thrilled. "It feels so good to do something about this instead of just watch the news and fume."

Nods all around; everyone felt good.

With the business aspects of the meeting concluded, Antoinette served the dessert she had made: a strawberry key lime tart.

Clandestine Delivery

Lilith and Mallory are going on a short trip to pick up more RU-486 pills – mifepristone – and deliver them to various locations.

Antoinette has given Mallory the money to buy them, as the pills must be sold to hospitals and physicians, not just any random person, and then dispensed to patients with a prescription.

Willow had made arrangements for them with the director of the place they would visit. She was in Paris with Antoinette and Manon and their fiancés.

Lilith was going with Mallory to help.

They wouldn't have to carry the pills anywhere.

All they had to do was use their wands to send them elsewhere, and they would be traveling by broomstick.

Lilith's fiancé and Mallory's boyfriend had not been told the purpose of this trip, but they knew better than to ask, and were proud of the witches.

They would fly by night only, so that meant staying a little while in each place.

It was evening, just after dark.

Lilith flew to Mallory's fire escape, let herself in, and found that Mallory was waiting for her.

"Do you need to do anything else before we go?"

"No," Lilith replied.

They said goodbye to Maleficent and Mallory's boyfriend, climbed out the window onto the fire escape, and flew off into the night.

Their destination was an unmarked building that belonged to Danco Laboratories. They had an appointment with the director.

It was a short ride as far as broomstick rides went. Remember, it had taken Lilith a couple of hours to get to Belgium, and this time, they were going to an undisclosed location in New York State.

The location of Danco Laboratories is a secret.

The reason for this is obvious: anti-abortion groups and individuals have committed, and continue to commit, murder of doctors, nurses, and anyone else who provides abortion assistance.

To protect the people who do the necessary work to make mifepristone available to women who need it, the location of the company's facility is not disclosed.

But witches can find anything.

The pills used to be manufactured in France, at a Paris pharmaceutical company called Roussel Uclaf

S.A. A scientist named Étienne-Émile Baulieu, Ph.D. developed the RU486 pill in 1980.

On May 16, 1994, the company donated manufacturing rights of the pill in the United States to the Population Council. In September of 1995, the Population Council licensed it to Danco Laboratories, which is in New York.

RU486 is the only drug that Danco manufactures, and it is heavily funded by private, pro-abortion, pro-choice donors. Antoinette is one of them.

It's a good thing that witches have always been on the side of women, particularly independent women. And witches are the epitome of independent women, because no one can tell them what to do and what not to do.

The meeting went smoothly.

The director, a woman who ardently believes in women's right to bodily autonomy and access to whatever is necessary to make that a reality, met them at the door roughly ten minutes after they took off from Mallory's fire escape.

She brought them into her office – which doubled as a library – and told them to go ahead and make themselves comfortable.

They took off their coats.

Lilith introduced herself and Mallory.

Hands were shaken, and water was offered.

"The guards are on the other ends of the property, as requested," the director told them.

"Good. Thank you," Lilith said.

But Mallory didn't want to linger here for long.

She was raring to go and get the pills on their way, plus see how Lilith had done this before and try it out herself.

The director therefore led them into the dimly lit, cavernous storage room of the facility.

"I didn't see your car," she said. "How are you going to transport the pills? And why do you have brooms with you?" she asked, looking puzzled.

"I'm a gynecologist, Lilith is an attorney, and we're both witches," Mallory told her.

Then the two of them took out their wands, levitated their broomsticks to a high shelf that couldn't be reached without a vertigo-inducing climb up a ladder, and put their wands back in their pockets.

The director stood there for a moment, speechless. Then she recovered and said, "So…will you be using magic to get the pills where they need to go?"

They grinned and nodded.

Lilith said, "We thought this would be more efficient if we told you up front what we are and then proved it with a little demonstration."

The director laughed. "You're right!"

She led them over to the boxes of RU486 pills.

"Should I not see how you do this?" she asked.

Mallory and Lilith laughed.

"You need to understand what happens to the pills, even if no one would believe you if you told them what you saw, so don't leave," Lilith said.

"Oh…okay," the director said, smiling.

Clearly, she was glad she would see magic.

With that, the wands came back out.

Mallory and Lilith were prepared with a list of GPS coordinates in their cell phones. Just as before, the phones themselves had had spells cast upon them to make tracking them impossible.

The pills were going to every state in the country, particularly the ones where abortion had been outlawed.

Mallory raised her wand and scrolled to the coordinates for a Jane doctor in Texas. Actually, she had a slew of Janes in Texas on her list.

"Texas," Lilith said. "That's a $100,000 fine for each flick of your wand."

Mallory gave her a diabolical grin and sent a box of pills to an undisclosed location in Texas.

Lilith scrolled to the top of her list of coordinates, raised her wand, and said, "Off to Florida with this box. This is cheaper: $5,000 for dispensing it, but it comes with a 5-year prison term."

The director looked angry about that.

"You two are so lucky you can fight back with just a flick of your wands," she said.

Mallory turned to her and said, "Gynecologists who don't have magic and live in pro-abortion states can fight by not putting their names on anything and sending it through a courier service. But not the U.S. Postal Service; they have sniffer dogs. Coffee beans don't always help; they're on to that tactic."

Lilith added, "We intend to save the Janes some of that trouble. This won't be our last visit here to do this."

The director nodded. She gave a little smile and said, "Thank you so much for doing this."

They nodded back. "Thank you, too!"

The witches kept working through their lists.

After about fifteen minutes, Janes in every anti-abortion state had received boxes of RU486.

"That's it. Done!" Mallory said. "Thank you for including me in this covert op and showing me how to do this," she said to Lilith.

The director looked at Lilith, realization slowly dawning on her. "That warehouse in Belgium…" she said, trailing off.

Lilith just grinned and said, "I have no idea what you are referring to."

The director nodded, but she was grinning.

With that, the witches levitated their brooms back down to their sides.

"It was lovely to meet you," Mallory said.

"Yes, quite lovely. You are another hero in this effort," Lilith added. "We hate to teleport boxes and run, but we really should go right back, so that we won't be missed."

"Yes," Mallory said. "For this clandestine delivery to seem not to have happened at all, we should be home as if we just went out for a brief visit together, nothing more, and can be back to work tomorrow as usual."

It was the director's turn to grin.

"Well then, I guess I can go home early!" she said. "This is great; I'll be back in time to watch Colbert."

It was only 10 p.m.

They women all walked outside.

The director's car was right outside, and the witches watched her open the driver's door and get inside.

Then they moved off to a dark area, away from the bright beams cast by the parking lot lights.

The director had started her car, but hadn't moved. She was watching them, too fascinated to drive off.

"I guess we can't blame her," Lilith said, straddling her broomstick.

"Nope, we can't," Mallory replied, doing the same thing.

They smiled and waved to the director and kicked off the ground.

As they rose into the darkness, the woman gaped at them. Then she seemed to have seen enough. She put the car in gear, backed out of her parking space, and drove off.

The witches turned toward New York City and flew through the night.

They too arrived home in time for Colbert.

Lilith had invited Mallory to spend the evening with her, and they found a nice surprise waiting at her place.

Lilith's fiancé liked to bake, and he made a nice batch of cranberry almond cardamom cinnamon oatmeal cookies.

They enjoyed the cookies with some raspberry hibiscus tea as they petted Nostradamus and watched their favorite comedian mock the orange fascist.

It felt so good to know that they had just come back from a successful and stealthy resistance mission as they watched the show.

Island Breezes

Antoinette was in Honolulu to perform with the Royal Hawaiian Band outside 'Iolani Palace. She had worked with them many times before, and always enjoyed it.

Manon had come with Antoinette on this trip.

It was just the two of them; their fiancés had to work, and so had stayed home to take care of the cats. Specter and Dauphine were used to this, and to them, so the dolls weren't worried about them.

Willow had done a good job with the accommodations; they were staying in one of the Beach Villas at the Ko Olina Resort on the western end of O'ahu.

The unit was a modern condominium, on the fourth floor of a section of the complex that faced the ocean. It had a kitchen, living and dining area, and two bedrooms, each with a full bathroom.

Sliding glass doors in the living room opened out onto a lanai with patio furniture. It was gorgeous.

The owner spent perhaps two weeks per year in this place, and rented it out the rest of the time. It was run like a hotel, complete with a cleaning staff.

Antoinette had plenty of space in which to practice her violin on her own, and she and Manon could cook if they wished to.

They had bought a week's supply of Kona coffee, and shipped several bags of it home to enjoy later. "My parents are going to be thrilled to get theirs," Antoinette said. "They loved this when they were here with me before."

Manon had promptly shipped some to her parents in Belgium with a note explaining what was so great about it. She was already addicted to it!

She had never been to Hawaii before, so she had taken her friend up on the chance to see 'Iolani Palace and tour the museums.

She went on the tour late on a Friday morning. The palace was beautiful despite having been emptied and used for much of the 20th century as office space. The curators had managed to recover a significant portion of the original furnishing and recreate the décor, which meant that visitors could get a sense of how everything had been when the Hawaiian royal family had lived there.

Manon enjoyed seeing the drawing room, which was furnished in royal blue with a lovely portrait of Queen Lili'uokalani.

Upstairs, she saw Queen Kapiolani's music room (the royal family was full of composers and musicians!), and a quilt that Queen Lili'uokalani had created while Hawaii was being stolen by the sons of the missionaries she had known from childhood.

Those men had grown up to found five large corporations, and they weren't going to let a thing such as Hawaii not belonging to them stop them from making a fortune.

At last, Manon emerged from the cellar, where she had just viewed the royal jewels.

The back door of the palace opened onto a parking lot with a sprawling, fantastic banyan tree.

The Royal Hawaiian band was on the lawn to the left, and Antoinette was out there with them. They were about to give their weekly Friday noon concert.

The concert began and ended with Queen Liliʻuokalani's song, "Aloha Oʻe" – which the queen called the "coming and going song." A hula dancer sang it as she moved beautifully in front of the orchestra.

Antoinette would be busy all week playing with them at various locations in Honolulu. She had seen all of the museums on the island on previous trips.

Manon was happy to listen to her at mealtimes as she told the curator all about them. She planned her time according to what her friend told her.

The next afternoon, she visited the Bernice Pauahi Bishop Museum. Just inside the front door, she saw a photograph of Princess Bernice with her husband.

The kahili collection was well worth the trip, and so was the main exhibit hall of the museum, which was three stories high, surrounded by balconies with more to see all around them.

Manon was having a wonderful time visiting Hawaii and learning about its culture. She even found out that Hawaiian women wear flowers – such as plumeria or orchids – on a different side of their heads depending on their relationship status.

She bought a beautiful clip with pink orchids on it. Because she had a fiancé, she put it in the left side of her hair. (Single women put it on the right.)

Hawaii was idyllic. It was a bit of a shock to experience how quickly night arrived, and how completely, though. Early in the evening, the sun would seem to go down the horizon rather abruptly. In just a matter of minutes, it was dark as night.

Of course, the place was well lit, so that didn't pose any logistical problems. In fact, there was much less ambient light and noise on this part of the island than in Waikiki, which was why Antoinette always stayed at the Ko Olina Resort.

Evenings were breezy but hot, so Manon was glad she had a cool nightgown to wear. She and Antoinette liked to sit out on the lanai in the evening and look at the ocean.

"Antoinette, do you think anyone in Hawaii will need Mallory's help? It's an awfully long way for her if they do…" Manon asked as they ate dinner on the third evening.

They had bought some scallops, a lime, butter, purple potatoes, and asparagus to cook, and coconut and mango ice cream for dessert.

"I doubt it," her friend replied. "The women of Hawaii don't have to worry about reproductive restrictions, thanks to state legislation that respects female bodily autonomy."

"Oh. That's good. I wish the United States had a pro-choice law for the entire country. Having it vary by state is terrible."

"Me too. France put it in its constitution. Here, getting an amendment for that would be extremely difficult, but it would be the best outcome. It's like our country is split in two over this issue. It's a lot like the Civil War, only this time, instead of slavery, it's reproductive rights."

The dolls got the small containers of ice cream out and took a scoop of each flavor. They sat back down at the table to enjoy it.

"It feels like another world here in Hawaii, away from all problems," Manon said.

"Oh, it has hurricanes, and debris from plastic polluters and disasters elsewhere, such as earthquakes, tsunamis, and nuclear accidents that washes up here. It just looks nice because we're at a resort."

Manon took that in and thought about it.

"Every place has its issues…" she said.

"It sure does."

Despite that, they enjoyed their time in Hawaii.

Ectopic Emergency

"Damn it!" Mallory said to herself after another emergency call on the Silphium Society hotline.

It was all very well to be helping women in trouble, but the trouble, Mallory found herself thinking yet again, was ridiculous.

A woman had an ectopic pregnancy and none of the hospitals in her area…nor her sister's, two states away from her home, would help her. The hospitals were religious and the doctors were trapped in anti-abortion states.

An ectopic pregnancy is one in a Fallopian tube.

If it wasn't removed, the woman would die.

The procedure for that is called a salpingectomy.

It was almost dark, fortunately, so travel would be fairly simple.

Mallory hopped onto her broomstick after a quick call to Lilith to tell her she needed help with her cat. Her friends were great about that.

Off she went into the night, heading for South Carolina.

Deonna was her patient's name. She was from Florida. She had gone to visit her sister, Jacee, after finding out that she couldn't get her Fallopian tube removed because the law there had scared the doctors out of helping her.

The women were poor and Black, and Deonna had taken an all-night bus ride to her sister's place near Greenville. She was exhausted and scared. So was her sister, but at least Jacee knew about the hotline and had called it.

They didn't know what else to do, and they lacked the financial resources to travel any further.

It took Mallory under half an hour to get there.

She landed, hopped off her broomstick, and glanced around.

It was a clear night, and she heard crickets and other nighttime sounds all around her.

She was in a dimly lit apartment area, on the edge of a parking lot, under a tree. No one was in the immediate area, but she could see people walking around in the distance.

A car pulled into the lot and a man parked.

He paid no attention to Mallory, but walked off toward one of the units to the right.

Mallory kept her broomstick with her and walked up to the apartment door. She could her female voices inside that sounded like the ones from the phone call. She knocked, and after a moment in which the peephole was used, the door opened.

She found the women in tears, and she didn't blame them…especially when she heard their story.

Deonna told her, "I couldn't just choose another doctor. And the one I saw told me that he wouldn't risk his medical license to abort this pregnancy. The nurse was furious. She told him that he was leaving me to die from it, but he didn't even care. He just said that that was the risk that women took when we have sex."

Mallory was incensed just to hear it.

Jacee said, "South Carolina isn't any better because religious hospitals control too much of abortion care."

After a brief examination of Deonna, she had made up her mind.

Mallory decided to take Deonna to a New York City hospital, where she had admitting privileges. 'I'll have to do the surgery tonight,' she thought to herself.

"Why are you carrying a broom with you?" Jacee asked suddenly, noticing it.

Deonna looked up at it, too, nonplussed.

Mallory sighed. "It's transportation."

She let that sink in.

It did, and the two sisters looked at her as if she were crazy.

She didn't have a lot of time to fool around because Deonna didn't, so she took out her wand and levitated dirty dishes into the sink, made the faucet go on, and caused the dish soap to rise, flip over, and squirt some soap onto a dish.

"If you believe me now, let's go," she said to Deonna. To both of them, she said, "This is an emergency. If you don't have that tube out quickly, you could die."

Jacee nodded, speechless. She hugged Deonna, handed her sister her purse and cell phone, and opened the door.

They all stepped out into the night and glanced around. No one was out, but some lights were on in windows nearby.

"Don't worry," Mallory said. "I've charmed them to not be paying attention."

Jacee and Deonna laughed with a hint of hysteria.

They were scared enough to be more concerned about Deonna's medical situation than anything else.

"Thank you for coming," Jacee said. "We really didn't think we had any options."

"I'm furious that women anywhere are backed into a corner like this," Mallory replied. "I didn't study and train to become a gynecologist to leave anyone to die. We're going to New York City."

With that, they stepped astride the broomstick, with Mallory steering in front and Deonna hanging on to her. "You won't fall off – I promise," Mallory said. "Just hang onto my waist and enjoy the view. We'll be there in about forty minutes."

Deonna did as she was asked and they took off.

Deonna was quiet, and in shock, no doubt, that she was actually a passenger on a witch's broomstick, which left Mallory to her thoughts.

As she flew north, Mallory found that her mind wouldn't stop dwelling on all of the legal data that Lilith had taught her.

Mallory had developed a working knowledge of abortion protections by state out of necessity. She liked to know where she was and was not protected, and her patients, too!

Shield laws had been enacted in many states – unfortunately states that were geographically far from yours – to protect women who need abortion care and their providing physicians. These were: California, Colorado, Connecticut, Delaware, Illinois, Maine, Maryland, Massachusetts, New York, Oregon, Rhode Island, Vermont.

Those states wouldn't share data about who did what: physicians giving abortion care, and patients receiving it, no matter where they are from. Also, physicians in their states were given protection against civil and criminal liability, professional discipline and protection related to liability, insurance, and health plans. In order words, everyone was covered.

Other states offered protections for abortion care but not for physicians: Arizona, Hawaii, Michigan, Minnesota, New Jersey, New Mexico, North Carolina, Pennsylvania, Washington (state), District of Columbia. More legal protections were needed in those states – the job wasn't done yet.

What was really needed was a national abortion law – one that gave women the right to an abortion on demand, no questions asked, with no punishments for their physicians and no insurance liabilities for giving abortions.

But meanwhile, Mallory wasn't waiting and watching anyone die due to the gap of time in abortion protection that misogynist legislators had caused.

They flew fast enough that it was like a video of landscape and illuminated cityscapes:

Charlotte, North Carolina.

Norfolk, Virginia.

Washington, D.C.

Philadelphia, Pennsylvania.

Atlantic City, New Jersey.

At last: New York City.

Mallory landed on her own fire escape.

They got off the broomstick and went through the window into her living room, where Maleficent sat on the top of the sofa, staring at them.

Deonna laughed. "Of course you have a black cat," she said.

Mallory grinned, put her broomstick in the closet, and asked if Deonna needed to pause to use the bathroom.

She did, and was quick.

Mallory had put her white medical coat on.

"Okay," Mallory said. "Onward; we're going outside on foot to get a cab to the hospital. The magical part of your medical rescue is over."

Deonna was actually starting to look happy.

No wonder; she had hope for a future again.

They went down in the elevator, walked outside, and Mallory hailed a cab. It took them out to 8th Avenue, up to 42nd Street, and across town to 1st Avenue. From there, it was a short length up to the Cornell University Medical College.

The cab dropped them off at the entrance to the emergency room, and Mallory quickly took charge.

"I'm Dr. Mallory Moonmist, and I have a patient here with a suspected ectopic pregnancy," she told the admitting nurse. "We'll need to do a scan to confirm this, and then likely take her in for immediate surgery."

They were waved on through, where Mallory oversaw two female gynecology residents as they conducted the examination. Yes, it was definitely an ectopic emergency.

The surgery went well.

Deonna came through with no complications. The salpingectomy went off perfectly, leaving her with the rest of her reproductive system intact.

When she woke up a few hours later, Mallory was there. "You did great," she told Deonna. "I've called your sister and told her so, too. Would you like to talk to her?" With that, she handed over her phone.

The sisters talked happily for a few minutes.

Then they ended the call, and Deonna handed back the phone.

"I don't know how to thank you," she said.

Mallory smiled. "Seeing you okay is thanks enough. I do have an unwritten prescription for you…and your sister: move to a pro-choice state."

Deonna nodded. "We were talking about that while you were on your way to us. I think we will do that soon. Jacee has some savings."

Mallory smiled. "If you have any trouble doing that, logistically or financially, call us again and we'll figure out a way to help. I'm not the only person who answers that number, and we have other people besides a gynecologist."

Deonna thanked her again and said she would.

With that, Mallory gave her hand a squeeze and left. She was ready to sleep this night off after two long flights, surgery, and everything else.

She went home, put on her pajamas, and curled up with her cat. Sleep came easily; she was tired out.

Children's Hospital Concert

Antoinette had laid out a new dress for Ileandra.

"What are these things?" the alien asked, scrutinizing the pattern on it.

"Lollipops," Antoinette told her. "They're sugar candy on sticks. Treats that many children enjoy. It's not great for their teeth, but it's a fun part of childhood. Lollipops come in fruit flavors, plus a few others."

"You want me to wear something that represents damage to children's teeth? Why?"

Antoinette smiled patiently. "Because it is a cheerful thing for children to think about, and we are going to entertain children today at a hospital. You did this with me before, and now we're going again, but to the Connecticut Children's Medical Center in Hartford."

"But why…why encourage them to ruin their teeth? Isn't that a crucial part of human health?"

"Yes, it is, but we have dentists and toothbrushes and dental floss to deal with all that, and enjoying sweets is one of life's great pleasures."

The alien looked at her skeptically.

Antoinette continued, "The reason why we are doing this is that a lot these kids are dying of cancer that human scientists aren't able to cure, so it won't matter if they wreck their teeth. The point is to make them happy while they're still alive, with as much fun as possible. Also, many aren't even allowed to eat lollipops, but they enjoy watching and listening to music about candy. I will be singing songs from movies based on a story by Roald Dahl called *Charlie and the Chocolate Factory*, among other candy-related music, so you will be helping me by wearing this. It will cheer the kids up to see that pattern on your dress, if only for a little while. It will also make their unhappy parents, who know what will happen to their kids later on, happy for a little while. Any happiness they can get is worth giving to them, since that's the best that we can do."

At last, the alien botanist understood. Ileandra put the dress on, smoothed her hair, and tied it in a bow with a matching ribbon, letting the ends hang down long in the back. She looked at Antoinette, standing in a corner of the room, then in the mirror.

Antoinette smiled. "Thank you for helping me," she said. She was already dressed for the event.

"You're welcome," Ileandra replied. "So…what do swans with crowns mean to children?"

Antoinette gave a brief laugh, then told her, "They mean fanciful fairy tales set to music and dance. I'll be playing Camille Saint-Saëns' "The Swan" from *The Carnival of the Animals*," some pieces from Pyotr Ilyich Tchaikovsky's ballet *Swan Lake*, and the musical score from a movie called *The Swan Princess* for them."

"That's perfect! What else will you play?"

"*The Sorcerer's Apprentice* by Paul Dukas and *Peter and the Wolf* by Sergei Prokofiev," Antoinette replied. "Those are reliable, classic pieces that children always like."

"And you have made something sweet…but you just said that the children are often not allowed to eat sweets. Who is this for?"

"This gingerbread bundt cake is for the nurses and other medical staff. I want to spoil them, too. They have to spend their careers on hopeless cases while trying not to get too attached to their patients. I just don't believe that it's possible to do that. It must be a depressing job, but they are such good and selfless people that they keep on doing it."

Ileandra listened to this with her huge eyes fixed on the violinist. Nothing like this was part of daily life on her planet. How could it be? They were tens of thousands of years ahead of Earth's history. But she knew that to get to the point that her people were at, they had once been like Antoinette's people.

She made no further comment as her Earth friend put the cake in a box. She just followed her out to the car, and off they went to entertain sick and terminally ill children.

On the way there, Antoinette sang the *Willy Wonka* song "Pure Imagination" for the alien, and then Ileandra rehearsed it with her. They would sing it together for the children.

"Remember," Antoinette warned, "smile as we sing. We're going there to give these kids a brief amount of happiness and fun. Don't look sorry for them. No crying. They know that they're doomed and that their health is failing. They don't need us to remind them of that. They need us to make them forget it while we're visiting them."

Ileandra listened gravely, and nodded. "I will smile, and keep a pleasant expression on my face as I listen to you play the rest of the music."

"Good. And thank you."

When the visit was over, Ileandra and Antoinette got into her car and drove back through Hartford, over Avon Mountain, and home to her house there.

Ileandra had a few questions as she rode along.

"How do children end up sick with cancer? It's the beginning of their lives. They haven't had time to eat the wrong things, get exposed to anything, or whatever else might cause such illnesses."

Antoinette glanced at her as she drove.

"Genetics play a role. It could be inherited."

"But humans now have the medical technology to test for that," Ileandra said, confused.

"Yes, we do, but the testing isn't perfect, and there are some religious people, even in the northeastern United States, who won't do it. They choose to have whatever baby comes along, regardless of the misery that that child will experience, or the expense incurred."

The alien stared at her in disbelief. "They choose this on behalf of their children?! And the children just have to be miserable because the parents can inflict their religious attitudes on them?!"

Antoinette gave a mirthless, wry grin. "Yes, they do that. Something is very wrong with that, and because people such as them are also elected to political office, it is very difficult to pass laws to stop that."

The alien was appalled.

Then she thought about visits to other children's hospitals that she and Antoinette had made, elsewhere in the country, the last time she had visited Earth and stayed with the violinist.

"What about other factors, such as environmental ones?" she wanted to know.

"Well…Connecticut doesn't have a lot of Superfund sites, so I guess it's mostly genetic cases that we're seeing here."

"What is a Superfund site?"

"It's a piece of land, usually right next to a residential area, where a factory that used chemical and biological toxicants once existed. It has been declared a mess by the federal government, and work done to clean it up…or not. The fund to clean it will hopefully get to it at some point, if not."

"And the children are sick because of it?"

"Yes. Well, in many places around the country, they are. Their mothers spend their pregnancies living there, drinking tap water that may be contaminated, and then they spend their babyhood and childhood there…and they end up sick because their families can't afford to live elsewhere. Moving costs a lot of money, and finding work elsewhere is often very difficult."

"That's terrible. And that's what my people went through, tens of thousands of years ago. I just didn't know the details, because it happened so long ago."

Antoinette glanced at her. They were at a stoplight. "Yes, well…you get busy living your present life, working hard, and you don't have time to think the past through like this unless you can simulate time travel by watching another planet's civilization experience what yours did, long ago."

Ileandra stared at her. "You would fit right in on my planet," she said. "It's good that Earth has you."

"Thank you for saying that. I hope this day has given you something to write about that your xenoanthropologist colleague will enjoy reading about."

"Oh! Yes, I definitely think so. Thank you for bringing me! I have definitely learned even more on this visit to a children's hospital than I did the last time I went to one with you."

Antoinette smiled. "I'm so glad you're here. I'll miss you when you go home."

"I'll miss you, too."

Tanglewood

Antoinette always looks forward to giving concerts at Tanglewood. It's a gorgeous estate in Lenox, Massachusetts, where the Boston Symphony Orchestra spends its summers.

This year was no different. Her concert was a Shakespeare-themed event. Playing at Seiji Ozawa Hall, a gorgeous, Japanese-themed venue with wood-paneling, Antoinette took the stage in the afternoon.

She played with the BSO, beginning with the orchestral score to the movie *Shakespeare in Love* by

Stephen Warbeck. It won the 1998 Academy Award for Best Original Musical or Comedy Score.

After the intermission, they play the orchestral score to *Much Ado About Nothing* by Patrick Doyle, from the 1993 movie.

The concert hall was full. Antoinette could see that the lawn beyond it, through the open back doors of the hall, has many blankets, picnic baskets, and lawn chairs filled with listeners enjoying the breeze and the music.

Antoinette finds it hot in late summer when she plays outside, and the concert halls at Tanglewood are open-air. As a result, she preferred to wear a white dress each time she performed there.

Her dress was a breathable cotton with an interwoven pattern of bees with floral wings. It has a full skirt with pockets, a sweetheart neckline, and puffed sleeves with lace on the cuffs. A satin ribbon in her favorite color, pastel pink, completes it.

Manon liked Antoinette's dress so much that she had had a similar one made for her wedding. The differences were that the satin sash was in Manon's favorite color, lavender, and the cloth had a different pattern, a floral. It was just what she wanted, pockets and all.

She wanted to get as much use out of it as possible, so she wore it at Tanglewood, but of course she didn't let on to her fiancé that she would be wearing this same dress with a different sash at their wedding!

Antoinette and Manon's fiancés thought that they looked so beautiful that they insisted on taking a photograph of them in the sunshine by the flower garden outside Seiji Ozawa Hall.

They had a very pleasant time at Tanglewood with their fiancés. The weather was clear, and although hot, up in the Berkshire Mountains, the temperature was at least manageable for the performers and concertgoers.

Ileandra Makes a Connection

Antoinette and Jasvinder had been hired to play at a formal ball in a private home. The owner of the home was a famous philanthropist, one who donated to liberal democratic causes.

Antoinette was very pleased to do this, not only for those reasons, but also because this person had contributed $10 million to the Silphium Society.

The house was in Greenwich, Connecticut.

That meant that when the event was over, they could go directly to Antoinette's Avon house, where her fiancé was with Specter the cat. There was also the convenient fact that several of Ileandra's fruit trees had been delivered. She could have them on her ship that very night.

Antoinette and Ileandra drove up from Manhattan, arriving at 5:30 p.m. The party would last until midnight.

At 6 p.m., a party guest brought Jasvinder. She had taken the train the day before to play at Yale University in New Haven.

When that concert ended, the guest, a professor of political science who had attended it, had graciously invited her to ride with him and his wife. Jasvinder had gladly accepted; she didn't feel safe using an Uber driver to get there. It could be anyone!

The hostess welcomed the three of them into the huge mansion, then brought them to a guest suite to relax, freshen up, and tune their instruments.

By 6:30 p.m., Antoinette and Jasvinder were quietly playing background music in a comfortable corner of the huge living room, which had an open kitchen overlooking it, and a bar off to the opposite side from where they sat.

Ileandra was given a fruit smoothie and left to wander freely around the room as the guests arrived.

She was wearing a formal black dress with a pattern of multi-colored alien environmental suit headpieces. She was determined to try again to get people to believe that she was from another planet.

Antoinette knew about this, and wasn't concerned. "Good luck," she had said.

The party guests consisted of wealthy donors to various causes, which pleased Antoinette and her friends, and famous professors, attorneys, scientists, and artists.

Some of them hovered around the musicians, waiting for them to take a brief break so they could chat. Antoinette and Jasvinder did pause now and then, and when dinnertime arrived, they switched off so that one of them was always playing.

Ileandra chatted with many of the people in attendance, but for much of the evening, she simply introduced herself as a botanist. That is, until one of them, another botanist, asked where she was based.

That was it. She told him the name of her planet.

"Is that a university? I've never heard of it."

"No. It's my planet. I'm here to get plants to grow in our depleted ecosystem."

The human botanist looked at her rather oddly.

Undeterred, Ileandra told him the name telepathically, with a view from space of her planet.

His eyes went wide with shock.

Ileandra just smiled, and then said, "Did you see how little green it has?"

He nodded, speechless.

"I have seen, while visiting Earth, that your planet and its people are, not all of you but definitely far too many of you, going through what mine did eons ago. If you don't change your collective resource use and reproduction rates, your planet will look a lot like mine…except for the shapes of the land masses."

"I'm so glad to have met you," the man said. "No one else will believe me, but I will work harder than ever now to impress the facts that you have shared me about our ecosystem's trajectory on people outside of academia."

Ileandra gave him a happy smile.

"Then my visit here this evening will have been worth it, and a success. It was wonderful to meet you!" she said.

Food Prices Up, Access Down

Antoinette and Ileandra were in Connecticut, shopping for groceries. They were preparing for a dinner party with Antoinette's parents, uncle, and fiancé.

They had a cart and a list.

Up and down the aisles, they filled the cart with the items on it, seeing noticeably higher prices.

Ileandra, concerned about access for the wider human population, was recalling her own people's past. But she didn't say this out loud to her friend; Antoinette had already heard about it.

However, Antoinette saw it and worried about hunger – not her own, as she could afford whatever food she wanted. She was concerned about other people, who couldn't.

When they got to the checkout counter, Antoinette donated the maximum amount suggested when she paid the bill.

Ileandra noticed that she did that at each of the grocery stores they shopped at: Big Y, the Fresh Market, and Whole Foods.

Antoinette noticed the alien noticing, and gave her a little smile. "I'm hopeful that the Herr Pumpkingropenfuhrer's determination to break everything will definitively break the economy, and thus his own following. His love of fake data that lies to him and the rest of us, with numbers that favor him, seems to be helping with this."

"It's terrible that that may just be what it takes to shock the majority of the voting public into wanting him out. But if so, bring it on," Ileandra agreed.

Neither of them looked forward to the misery that many households would face in order to make that a reality, though.

"Farmers and agribusinesses and immigrants who pick produce are all being attacked. Everyone loses," Antoinette said as they drove from Big Y to Whole Foods. "The immigrants who work as pickers are doing jobs that Americans don't want, yet they are being rounded up and arrested. Agribusinesses are trying to poison all weeds, and just end up ruining crops and pushing independent farmers out."

Ileandra sat in the passenger seat, listening.

She said, "We used to have those same conditions in our food system. That's how I ended up with a botany career that involves travel to other planets to forage for non-genetically modified organic food. I got extremely lucky when I met you," she summed up.

Antoinette smiled as she parked the car.

"Here we go to a store that has another name: the 'Whole Paycheck.' That's because it was already more expensive than regular grocery stores."

"What made it more expensive?"

"Non-GMO produce."

The alien was aghast, but not really surprised.

In they went with the next list.

Antoinette bought a wheel of Brie and some Belgian lambic beer – raspberry and strawberry. She also bought some claret wine, imported from France.

After a quick turn down the baking aisle for chocolate and sliced almonds, they paid and got back into the car,

Next, they went to the Fresh Market for coffee.

"I love their coffee," Antoinette said. "So does my aunt in Newport, Rhode Island. "For some reason, she can't get Southern Pecan coffee where she lives, so I buy it here whenever I go to visit her."

Ileandra nodded and watched as Antoinette bought some of that for later, plus some Toasted Almond Crème coffee, and some Mocha Java. She ground the flavored beans in the machine to the right, and the Mocha Java beans in the left one.

"The Mocha Java is for my uncle and parents," she told the alien.

Ileandra noticed that her friend had started with Big Y, a "regular" grocery store, and bought almost everything on her list there.

"Having plenty of money is no excuse for shopping like I don't need that store," Antoinette said. "It needs the business from everyone to keep prices from getting even worse."

The alien nodded, and settled in for the ride back to the house, where they unpacked everything and set the table for dinner.

Soon, Antoinette was busy baking a brie en croûte with red raspberry preserves while she made a salad with chevre, pistachio nuts, craisins, fresh greens, multi-hued cherry tomatoes, scallions, and red, orange, and yellow bell pepper chunks.

The main meal would be orange saffron shrimp
with basmati saffron rice.

When the brie came out of the oven, it was a
thing of beauty, with the raspberry jam swirled all
through it.

Dessert was a chocolate torte with chocolate
curls and toasted almonds. Antoinette seemed to
forget her life as she worked on it; the alien could
sense that telepathically as she watched her friend.

A little while later, the family arrived, and
everyone had a pleasant evening…even though
Antoinette's mother and uncle discussed food prices
at some length. They, too, were well-aware of the
effect of the senseless policies of fascism.

Diwali Disquietude

It was Diwali, the time of the Hindu festival of light, and everything should be happy, hopeful, and enjoyable. It was a 5-day tradition that celebrated the goddess Lakshmi, and the triumph of good over evil.

But it didn't feel that way.

Jasvinder was having some trouble with her travel arrangements for a concert at the Metropolitan Opera that she and Antoinette had planned.

Willow had booked everything for her, and she could stay with Antoinette at her Manhattan apartment. The Pumpkingropenfuhrer administration had caused Jasvinder (along with all other travelers!) problems with her visa.

Fees and wait times had increased exponentially; the visa processing fees were up by 300 percent. She would make less of a profit on her concerts due to overall costs of roughly $10,000, so staying with Antoinette helped to shave off some of the expense. She was glad they were longtime friends.

But the processing times had her worried. Expediting the process drove the cost up, but it seemed to work. Either way, it involved detailed documentation and a mandatory interview at a U.S. consulate each and every time she was to travel to America.

It was exhausting, and felt like a major imposition on her time – time that she should have had to spend practicing her sitar and resting up for the trip.

Dinner had been an hour ago, and she should have been calmly looking forward to the evening with her family, but no…she had come back upstairs to check all these details, including the appointment for the interview at the U.S. consulate, which was the next afternoon.

Jasvinder's sister had been enjoying watching people set off firecrackers in the neighborhood as the Diwali festivities went on. Suddenly, her sister came upstairs and dragged her outside, saying, "Good – you already have your Diwali-themed sari on. Let's go! You need a break."

The cat, Sita, smiled at her and curled up for a nap, oblivious to the racket. More firecrackers went off. The cat's eyes opened, but that was all; they closed again.

"I don't know how that cat can sleep now," Jasvinder said to herself, leaving the room.

The sisters went downstairs, where their parents waited for them with chai and sweets. The table was laid out with a special spread of all sorts of treats, and candles lit the room.

When they were done eating and drinking everything, the daughters cleared everything up while their parents extinguished the candles.

Then they all got into the car and drove to the waterfront for a fireworks show. Everywhere they went along the way was lit up. The city looked particularly beautiful.

Jasvinder decided to enjoy the evening, and not let Herr Pumpkingropenfuhrer live rent-free in her head, as Antoinette called that state of mind.

The family enjoyed their evening out.

The Metropolitan Opera

Along with the Metropolitan Opera and its orchestra, Antoinette had planned a benefit concert to help make up the shortfall in funding for PBS that the Herr Pumpkingropenfuhrer administration had caused.

It was also to include a ball after the concert.

Antoinette had arranged the music: a medley of tunes from regular PBS programming, including the theme from *Mystery!* – complete with the Edward Gorey cartoon playing on a screen overhead.

Jasvinder was there to play her sitar. She had prepared a segment of ragas, and would sing in Hindi and in English. (Her fiancé had flown over from India with her, on a tourist visa.)

The other dolls had all turned out in their formal gowns to attend in support of this effort. They were enjoying the chance to visit with each other again.

Outside, the modern façade of the Met was lit up beautifully. Ileandra was fascinated by the water fountain. "We don't dare enjoy water that way on my planet," she said in a wistful tone.

Nichelle and Willow looked at her, but made no comment. They were thinking about what it must mean to live in a severely depleted ecosystem…everywhere on one's planet.

The other dolls had gone inside to see the famous red-carpeted staircase and curved balconies of the Met's lobby.

The chandeliers resemble starbursts, and when the others joined them, the alien was quite impressed by them. "They look almost like the beautiful views we enjoy out our ship windows," she said.

Willow and Nichelle envied her the chance to see that and see that often, but they were nevertheless glad to remain on Earth with its still-verdant biome.

Lilith, Mallory, and Manon (in her classic little black dress, channeling Coco Chanel) listened to the alien and had similar thoughts…also unspoken.

The ushers rang their chime, sounding an arpeggio of A, C, and E notes, and they all went in to take their seats.

Antoinette, accompanied by Jasvinder, walked out onto the stage to say a few words.

"Thank you all for coming to this special concert to fund the Public Broadcasting System. The proceeds from this performance will be used to create an endowment that will benefit stations all across the United States. This concert will also be recorded and shared with every PBS station. I will be playing my violin, and my friend and colleague from Mumbai, India, Jasvinder Lakshmi Shivdasani, will be playing her sitar."

With that, the concert commenced.

The theme music for *Masterpiece Theater* was played first, appropriately enough, since it runs during the opening credits for that show. It is the Fanfare-Rondeau from *Suite of Symphonies for brass, strings and timpani No. 1* by French composer Jean-Joseph Mouret.

Not to be omitted, the *Mystery!* theme with its accompanying Edward Gorey cartoon came next. (Antoinette admitted it later, just to her friends: she was very excited about this, and it was worth it. The audience cheered and clapped!)

Antoinette smoothly transitioned from playing various themes from mystery shows such as *Midsommer Murders*, *Foyle's War*, and Agatha Christie's *Murder on the Orient Express* movie (the one with Albert Finney as Hercule Poirot, co-starring Sean Connery) to children's Head Start shows such as Sesame Street.

All were projected onto the screen above the stage, complete with Julia, the autistic Muppet. Antoinette spent a lot of time arranging this with someone from New York City's NPR station and someone from the opera house.

Theme tunes from *Rick Steves' Europe*, *Antiques Roadshow*, *All Creatures Great and Small*, and *Downton Abbey* followed. Antoinette sang "Did I Make the Most of Loving You?" by the composer John Lunn and Don Black for that last one, in a quiet, haunting voice, just as it was meant to be sung.

Antoinette and Jasvinder played the theme music composed by George Fenton from *The Jewel in the Crown*, a series about the last days of the British Raj.

Next came Alexander Faris's theme music for *Upstairs, Downstairs*.

Those of the dolls who hadn't been to the Metropolitan Opera before enjoyed the venue as well as the performance. They also enjoyed meeting the celebrities and wealthy donors.

Nichelle made the most of her opportunity to chat with the donors. She was as determined as ever to continue all of her work uninterrupted, and meeting these people in person helped.

Lilith simply introduced herself as an attorney for the Silphium Society, and then explained its mission and work. Mallory was alongside her, and Lilith explained that she answered the hotline calls. She told people nothing about what Mallory did when she finds out what the callers needed, and no one asked. That was confidential, between the doctor and patient – legally privileged communication.

The witches' pockets were stuffed with business cards for the Silphium Society, and of course they had their wands.

Manon was already well known to the attendees, thanks to her work in both New York City and Paris. Lots of these people spent money at Christie's auction house and visited the Louvre.

Willow was introduced as the accountant, which did not excite much interest beyond filling her gown's pockets up with business cards, but she was very happy to collect them.

Ileandra realized that, as this was the last social event she would attend on this trip to Earth, she might as well enjoy the intermission and afterparty by outing herself yet again as an alien.

Antoinette had had the ideal gown made for Ileandra on this occasion, with a star pattern on shades of blue. Ileandra loved it, and it made her presentation easier.

Of course, so did her telepathy, now that she had figured out that the best approach was to tell people who and what she was and then project the images of her depleted planet telepathically. She had lots of fun surprising people.

The wealthy donors were so amazed, delighted, and impressed that evening that they gave more money to both NPR and the Silphium Society. They welcomed any suggestions from Nichelle, too, and had their assistants take notes.

Ileandra was bemused to see that these people went out and about with assistants to do their bidding. But it did make things happen, and with ruthless efficiency!

The performance and the afterparty together proved to be a great success. Everyone enjoyed the music and the conversation at the gathering.

Antoinette and Jasvinder's fiancés both had beautiful bouquets for them. It was pink roses with purple lilacs and blue irises for Antoinette, and jasmine with pink lotus flowers for Jasvinder – their favorites.

Ileandra Leaves

The last of the plants that had been ordered for Ileandra had been delivered to Antoinette's house in Avon, Connecticut.

It was time for the alien to leave. Her memoir was fully drafted, and Antoinette had the fictitious version of it almost ready to publish.

Antoinette, Jasvinder, and Willow were there to see her off, complete with a going-away party.

During the day before Ileandra's departure, some surprises arrived: butterfly bush, a pastel pink peony root, and two rose bushes – one pastel pink and the other red.

Antoinette grinned as she presented them.

"You can make rosewater, and also just enjoy the blossoms on the plants. And you can use the peony flowers the same way. I use rosewater in desserts, which you have tasted. Now you can, too."

Ileandra was thrilled! "Thank you very, very much!" she said, hugging her friend. "I didn't want to ask for any…recreational plants, but I am very excited to have these!"

Antoinette, Willow, and Jasvinder laughed.

"Recreational…" Antoinette said, trailing off. "Enjoyment of what plants can bring you is one of the best things about being alive."

The alien nodded.

Jasvinder chimed in, "That was a loaded statement. There are some Hollywood…and Bollywood…stars who enjoy certain other recreational plants."

Willow giggled. "Pot – marijuana," she said, when the alien looked puzzled.

"Oh…right," Ileandra said, laughing. "Those, I think, would be too intense for me and my people."

"I thought as much," Antoinette said, laughing with her. "Coffee is something you have to be careful with, so of course pot would be even more of an issue," she added, seeing Ileandra looking at her, surprised.

Ileandra got it then. "You're right."

Everyone laughed, and then went quiet. It was getting dark.

"I'm going to miss you – a lot," Antoinette said.

"So am I," Willow and Jasvinder chorused.

"And so will Manon and Lilith. They said they were sorry they couldn't be here to see you off."

"I'm going to miss all of you, too," Ileandra said. They all hugged.

"Will you visit again?" Antoinette had to ask.

"If you will have me, I will be glad to come back. Who else will let me follow them around as they go about their life and supply me with plants but my friends here?" Ileandra replied.

"Oh, we'll be happy to do it again," Jasvinder said. "Visit me again, too! I'm sure we can keep thinking of more plants to give you."

Willow said, "And you don't even need my help with travel arrangements."

"You never know about that. You can help me plan logistics for when I beam down."

With that, she beamed up, and was gone.

The Resistance Continues…

The Silphium Society's work would continue.

Herr Pumpkingropenfuhrer was going to be around for the foreseeable future.

So were the radical Christian nationalist fascists who were determined to make life for women as constrained as possible.

Every day, they could be quoted as having said the most offensive, infuriating things about women's bodily autonomy.

Turning the clock back on women's rights was their fondest wish. Attacks on access to birth control were being planned in forced birth state legislatures.

Antoinette had arranged another meeting at her house, and everyone had gone outside for some fresh air. They needed it after watching the news reports on MS NOW.

The dolls were furious, as were American women. But at least they had a way to do something about it.

"It's always angry, low-I.Q. men with inferiority complexes who do this," Antoinette griped. "They think that by taking rights and access to what makes bodily autonomy possible for women, they will gain something that is missing in their own lives."

"They won't," Lilith said, "and there will always be hateful individuals out there. It's why I carry my wand around at all times, even when we have a liberal government. If there is a shooter and I can disarm the lunatic, I can and will."

Antoinette recalled that Lilith had done just that on the previous Juneteenth.

Mallory said, "I hope the Silphium Society's coffers are growing ever deeper, in case of legal problems for Janes who can't do magic. Sooner or later, one will be detected, and we'll be reading about her in *Abortion, Every Day* and hearing about her on the news. As it is, we already hear about some."

Willow assured her that the coffers were comparable to an abyss.

Mallory grinned.

The others were listening.

Nichelle spoke after a moment.

"Mallory, when this all started, I couldn't believe that you were serious about using your broomstick. I'm sorry I looked at you like you were crazy or something. It's just that I had no idea that witches existed outside of books."

"That's okay! It's better that way," Mallory replied with a smile.

"Yes," Lilith said. "No one will believe you anyway if you tell them." She was smiling, too.

Jasvinder had to add, "We wouldn't be believed if we told anyone about our friend the alien botanist, either."

Everyone laughed; that was true.

"Where do you think the United States is going with its problems?" Jasvinder asked.

"We're as divided over fascism and reproductive rights in the early 21st century as we were over slavery in the mid-19th century," Antoinette said. "Look at where that got us then: the Civil War of 1861-1865."

"What will happen next?" Willow asked, horrified at the implications of that and looking at Lilith. "You're the lawyer of our group. What do you think? Will American democracy reset itself?"

Lilith looked more serious than ever. "We hope so, but only time will tell. But look at the outcome of the Civil War: slavery ended, and democracy continues to struggle even now."

"Until then, we must keep fighting for women's independence, and take it wherever it is blocked, withheld, or otherwise stolen," Antoinette said. "Laws that don't respect our bodily autonomy shall not be respected back!

Everyone agreed.

The Silphium Society would continue to fight.

About the Photographs

The majority of the photographs that appear in this book are my own.

This includes all of the doll images.

After I completed each doll outfit, I dressed the doll and posed her on a neutral, all-blue background with a blue wall and blue blanket, fussed over every hair on her head, the pose of the doll, and the outfit to make sure that everything was in place. Then I took her photograph for this book.

I have a large personal collection of photographs from travel and other events which I have drawn on in order to place each doll in a background that is suitable to whatever she is doing in the story. This is accomplished via Photoshop, combining the images.

In a few instances, this has not been possible, so I found others on Wikimedia Commons, and placed the dolls in them. The photographers, but they don't all want to reveal their names. Read the credits to see some funny fake names that they chose!

Image credits:

1. "One story building flooded after Hurricane Katrina, S. Carrollton Avenue, Mid City New Orleans. Flood water high water mark visible." October 14, 2005. Photograph by Infrogmation. Wikimedia Commons, https://en.wikipedia.org/wiki/File:SCarrollton1Floor.jpg. Page 45.

2. Stained glass planet: 1.75 inches in circumference; one-of-a-kind, called "Possibly Inhabited Little Planet," by Josh Simpson of *Josh Simpson Glass*, https://www.joshsimpsonglass.com/ Page 92.

3. "New Orleans - St. Louis Street at Dauphine Street, downtown river corner, French Quarter." April 16, 2023. Photograph by Eden Pictures. *Wikimedia Commons*, https://commons.wikimedia.org/wiki/File:Cast-Iron_Balconies,_New_Orleans_French_Quarter,_April_2023.jpg. Page 135.

4. "Walt Disney Concert Hall." August 7, 2006. Photograph by Kelvin Kay. *Wikimedia Commons*, https://commons.wikimedia.org/wiki/File:Disneyconcerthall2.jpg. Page 136.

5. "Interior of the Millennium Biltmore Hotel." February 25, 2016. Photograph by P.G. Roy Photography. *Wikimedia Commons*, https://commons.wikimedia.org/wiki/File:Interior_of_the_Millennium_Biltmore_Hotel-24651397143.jpg. Page 137.

6. "Christie's, 20 Rockefeller Plaza, Manhattan, New York." June 4, 2014. Christie's is the world's largest art business and a fine arts auction house. Photograph by Leonard J. DeFrancisci. *Wikimedia Commons*, https://commons.wikimedia.org/wiki/File:Chris

tie%27s_(Manhattan,_New_York)_001.jpg. Page 182.

7. "Palais Royale." Flowerbed with flowering irises in the Tuileries Garden in Paris in springtime. June 7, 2013. Photograph by Michelle Maria. *Wikimedia Commons*, https://commons.wikimedia.org/wiki/File:Palais_Royale_-_panoramio_(16).jpg. Page 220.

8. "The Large Staircase of The Garnier Opera, in Paris." This image consists of 12 photographs, stitched together with Hugin. Each photo was taken by hand, hence the lack of details. Paris, France; July 29, 2007: Photograph by unnamed person. *Wikimedia Commons*, https://commons.wikimedia.org/wiki/File:Opera_Garnier_Grand_Escalier.jpg. Page 221.

9. "Shamrai E.A., a member of expedition 'Arctic Floating University 2013' during the night. On board the research vessels Professor Molchanov's scientific work was conducted around the clock. Picture taken during the project 'The Arctic floating university'". It is an innovative educational project designed to help young scientists - explorers of the Arctic receive knowledge and skills in real life conditions of the northern seas." June 16, 2003. Photograph by Shammray. *Wikimedia Commons*, https://commons.wikimedia.org/wiki/File:Polar_night.jpg. Pages 207 and 251.

10. "Street food vendors in Panaji, Goa, India." July 8, 2023: Photograph by Radosław Botev, *Wikimedia Commons*, https://commons.wikimedia.org/wiki/File:Street_food_vendors_in_Panaji,_Goa.jpg. Page 224.

11. "Road in the Interior of Sanjay Gandhi National Park." It is the only national park of Mumbai and is well known for its flora and fauna. August 8, 2014. Photograph by Aalokmjoshi, *Wikimedia Commons*, https://commons.wikimedia.org/wiki/File:Road_inside_SGNP_03.jpg. Page 232.

12. "Staircase between decks, portside, T.S.S. *Earnslaw*, Lake Wakatipu, New Zealand." January 19, 2004. Photograph by Bluedawe. *Wikimedia Commons*, https://commons.wikimedia.org/wiki/File:Stairway_TSS_Earnslaw.jpg. Page 258.

13. "Whole Foods Market." July 4, 2013. Photograph by Fastily. *Wikimedia Commons*, https://commons.wikimedia.org/wiki/File:Whole_Foods_2_2013-07-04.jpg. Page 310.

14. "Gateway of India located on the waterfront in the Apollo Bunder area in South Mumbai and overlooks the Arabian Sea." Before November 6, 2016. Photograph by Alok Kumar, *Wikimedia Commons*,

https://commons.wikimedia.org/wiki/File:Gate way_Of_India_(181539875).jpeg. Page 317.

15. View of the proscenium arch at the Metropolitan Opera House, Lincoln Center for the Performing Arts, New York City, June 30, 2009. Uploaded by Ser Amantio di Nicolao, *Wikimedia Commons*, https://commons.wikimedia.org/wiki/File:Metr opolitan_Opera_curtain.jpg. Page 318.

16. "The facade of the Metropolitan Opera House at Lincoln Center, New York, New York." June 30, 2007. Photograph by Blehgoaway. *Wikimedia Commons*, https://commons.wikimedia.org/wiki/File:Facad e_of_the_Metropolitan_Opera_House_at_Lincol n_Center,_NYC.jpg.

17. "Metropolitan Opera House Stairway." August 4, 10`7. Photograph by Marco Almbauer. *Wikimedia Commons*, https://commons.wikimedia.org/wiki/File:Metr opolitan_Opera_House_staircase.jpg.

Acknowledgements

There are some people I have to thank for making this book a reality.

My father gave me a Nikon camera and taught me how to use it. He also listened as I read the chapter about violins to him and commented helpfully about the quality of the sounds that different sizes of Stradivarius violins offer.

My grandmother, Anna Ruth Baker Fox, taught me how to sew when I was eleven years old.

My Aunt Joan Fox, an artist who studied at the Rhode Island School of Design, was happy to offer encouragement and view each doll outfit. Thank you for helping me decide which fabric patterns were best! She also helped me as I finished embroidering each doll's face. Her comments about the eyes showed me how to get the facial expressions right.

My mother bought me a sewing machine during the pandemic, which got me started sewing. She was endless fun to discuss this project with and show the dolls to in their dresses, and to bounce ideas off of.

She also encouraged me and steered me as I embroidered Ileandra's eyes, to make sure that they looked as they should. We were both pleased with the result. For this doll book, she guided me on enhancing the makeup of the dolls' eyes, and the result was well worth it.

My mother found this project exciting as she watched each doll brought down the runway to be viewed. She also edited the manuscript, because no author can find their own errors! Thank you, Mommy!

My uncle, Douglas A. Conant, and my friend, Adam M. Frost of computer care and learning (he is not a fan of capital letters!), taught me most of what I know about using a computer.

All of these people enabled me to create the dolls and this book, and it was a thrill to bring all of these aspects of my life together.

About the Desserts

The desserts that appear in this book are my own.

I love to bake – to make a work of edible art out of a dessert – and then to memorialize my creation in a photograph before cutting into it and eating it.

Recipes include ones that I love from cookbooks, plus some that I have tweaked just for the fun of it to make them unique and with a different flavor.

Some recipes are even ones that I created myself. It's part of the fun of life to make these things and spoil the people I care about with homemade, gourmet desserts, such as this orange star-bundt cake with orange glaze.

Background on the Dolls

My mother, who can always be counted upon to stop at a tag sale, noticed Mr. Guilmartin's yard was laid out with an enticing array of antiques and other intriguing items. Among them were little witches' broomsticks. We bought a set of 3 for a dollar.

Frank Pannenborg, my father's college friend, was visiting with us that day. He likes to see people's projects, so when I made my first witch, Mallory, I e-mailed him a photograph.

He replied with a bit of character background on her, saying "She's a very sweet witch – probably had a hard time socially in witch school." She did come out with a slightly anxious facial expression. I have since re-embroidered her face, but a bit of that expression still remains.

With that, an idea began to form in my mind: why not have fun making more dolls? I could create 3 witches, improve my sewing skills, and finally figure out how to make beautiful, comfortable dresses with pockets…in miniature.

Antoinette had been built up in my imagination over the past couple of decades – maybe even longer. For her, I sent Frank some details on her character background. She was mine to fill out the back-story of!

From there, I was off, creating 2 more characters.

After I finished them, and finished outfitting them, I knew I hadn't gotten enough of that, so I created 5 more dolls.

The fabrics came from Joann, Etsy, Amazon, and Spoonflower.

Spoonflower is a fascinating source of material because artists from all over the planet upload their patterns to its website, carefully configured to repeat seamlessly once printed onto whatever variety of cloth is desired. I learned what it is like to work with cotton poplin, cotton jersey, cotton lawn, and petal signature cotton. Each one has a different feel to it.

The artists whose designs appear on the Spoonflower website make some gorgeous images, and some fascinating ones. My favorite is Utart by Uta Haumann, but others that I like are: Thistle and Fox, Rachel Quinlan, Weaving Major, M to the Fifth Power, Simone Balman, 3rittanyLane, Peacoquette Designs, Chelsea Rockey Graphic Design, Hip Kid Designs, Charlotte Winter, Flowers for Bear, AngelGer28, Coffee and Pixels, Simpson Design Studio, Andrus Gardens, Mirabelle Print, Nickleen, Space Oleandr, Nemki, Lily Sabbagh Design, Episodic Drawing by Lea Yunk, Goldie Winship, Yvonne Hart Studio, Shop Cabin, Studio Tuesday, Natalia Ruzhyna Artist, 13 Rapports by Lena Nasmi, Designs by Adenaj, Astro Felis, Miriam Kokolo, SomeCallMeBeth, Mariden, Ilustrinna, Lierre, Punky Pink Cow, and Misentangled Vision.

On Etsy, a brand of fabric called Timeless Treasures makes the most wonderfully soft cotton in a fascinating and beautiful array of patterns. For Jasvinder's sari fabrics, I found Etsy shops that offered block-printed cotton made in India, which was sent to me from there. The sellers saw her when

I messaged them to explain why I didn't want to buy 5 metres of cloth, and were delighted by her.

Designing the outfits was a lot of fun. Sometimes I learned by accident how to make an element of a dress that I had liked. Other times, I watched a YouTube video to learn a technique. Staring at images on Pinterest helped, too.

The next part of my addictive routine was photographing the dolls in each outfit.

My mother got in on the process by photographing me holding each doll.

I have enjoyed it all to the point that I was sorry to finish this project. So sorry, in fact, that I decided to do it again, and this book is the result.

Details of the Dolls

Each of these dolls has her names written in Chancery Italic calligraphy on her left ankle, and **QueenBeeDoll**, a logo, on her butt (left side).

Their faces, ears, earrings, and manicures were stitched with cotton stranded mouliné embroidery threads. Their hair then sewn onto their heads, concealing the knots from the entry of the embroidery needle.

Doll hair can be found from various sources: American Girl Doll supplies, Amazon, Factory Direct Craft, and Etsy.

Lilith
Hermione
Wandcraft

Ileander

The Author with Her Dolls

This doll-making fun began with a tag sale that sold me at set of 3 miniature broomsticks for a dollar. I decided to make a witch.

That witch is Dr. Mallory Miranda Moonmist.

She got the purple broomstick. I embroidered her rather clumsily, though, and was not ready to show her in a book, so I tried harder with the next doll, determined to do better.

Antoinette was the result. She was a character who had been built up in my mind for over two decades, and she came out, amazingly enough to me, pretty much as I had envisioned her.

From there, I had to learn to make doll clothes.

I watched YouTube and made patterns. It took some false starts and stops, but I figured it out, using up the rectangles of fabric that remained from the pandemic and mask-making.

If I made mistakes, I thought, what had I lost? Just a little bit of fabric. No problem!

Meanwhile, I published my first doll book, *Antoinette: A Year in the Life of a Doll with Her Friends*, and kept going. It was just too much fun to stop!

I had a jumper and a dress from a craft fair; I converted them to skirts and used the tops for dresses for Lilith and Manon.

Manon was created by accident. She was a blank doll that I used as a fitting mannequin. I found myself calling her Manon the Mannequin, and soon I was creating another character.

After that, I plucked out Mallory's stitches, re-embroidered her face properly, and cut her loose from her broomstick. She was now a doll as well as a witch, and another character.

Jasvinder was to be a friend for Antoinette from music school. Now I was in for another challenge: dying the doll.

I might as well do that all at once, I thought, because I also wanted a Black doll, and I had lots of ideas for her career. Nichelle is named after the *Star Trek* actress and a journalist-suffragist, Ida Bell Wells. More YouTube videos!

First Jasvinder with a Rit brand dye, then Nichelle with a darker hue, and then a cycle in the dryer. I worried about getting them completely dry, but I needn't have, because – it worked! And the dolls were perfectly dry all through.

Then I had to learn to make a choli (close-fitting blouse), a ghagra (skirt), and a sari (long rectangle of cloth), and then put it all together on Jasvinder. Pin the folded end of the sari for a pallu to hang over her shoulder, then fold, tuck, fold, tuck, fold, tuck.

I loved figuring it all out, and Etsy sold lots of beautiful cotton block-printed fabrics.

Willow was created because I wanted an eighth doll (something about that number draws me to it), and because I found a pretty doll wig on ebay for 99 cents. It was too good a deal to pass up.

Even better, I found myself creating a character who reminds me of my best friend from college, Beth. Willow and Beth like the color blue and Japanese art, and they have accounting degrees.

Beth, however, is American, not Canadian. I didn't make a clone of my friend; the doll was merely inspired by her.

With eight dolls and a plot for another story in mind, I was back at it, making more beautiful dresses, and branching out to try using different varieties of fabrics.

Soon I had outfits for another book.

After months of sewing outfits for my dolls, I realized that I knew enough to be able to make clothing for humans. Also, the dolls could have dresses from the remnants.

This is endless fun, and I have continued sewing, making holiday and birthday blouses for my friends and relatives.

My mother now has pajamas, a nightgown, and a blouse. My aunt has two summer and two winter nightgowns and several blouses and shirts. My friends have blouses.

Best of all, I am happy because the fashion industry has always frustrated me. If it sells something with beautiful floral patterns, I am delighted…but never for long, because the fashions for women constantly change. And pockets aren't always offered in our clothing, which is a source of aggravation to me. But I can sew now, so that means pockets and control of the fabrics and styles. At last, I feel in control of clothing and enjoy it.

Many of the fabrics I have used to sew outfits for my dolls come from Spoonflower, which sells cloth by the yard. It takes half a yard to make most doll dresses, so I shall be making more to sell to people who want to enjoy these beautiful patterns.

My dolls are 18 inches tall, and about the size of American Girl Dolls, if that helps you to get a sense of the size and fit of the dresses I make.

If you want me to make a dress for your doll, please visit my doll shop on Etsy at https://queenbeecouturiere.etsy.com

Antoinette and Stephanie

Lilith and Stephanie

Mallory and Stephanie

Manon and Stephanie

Jasvinder and Stephanie

Nichelle and Stephanie

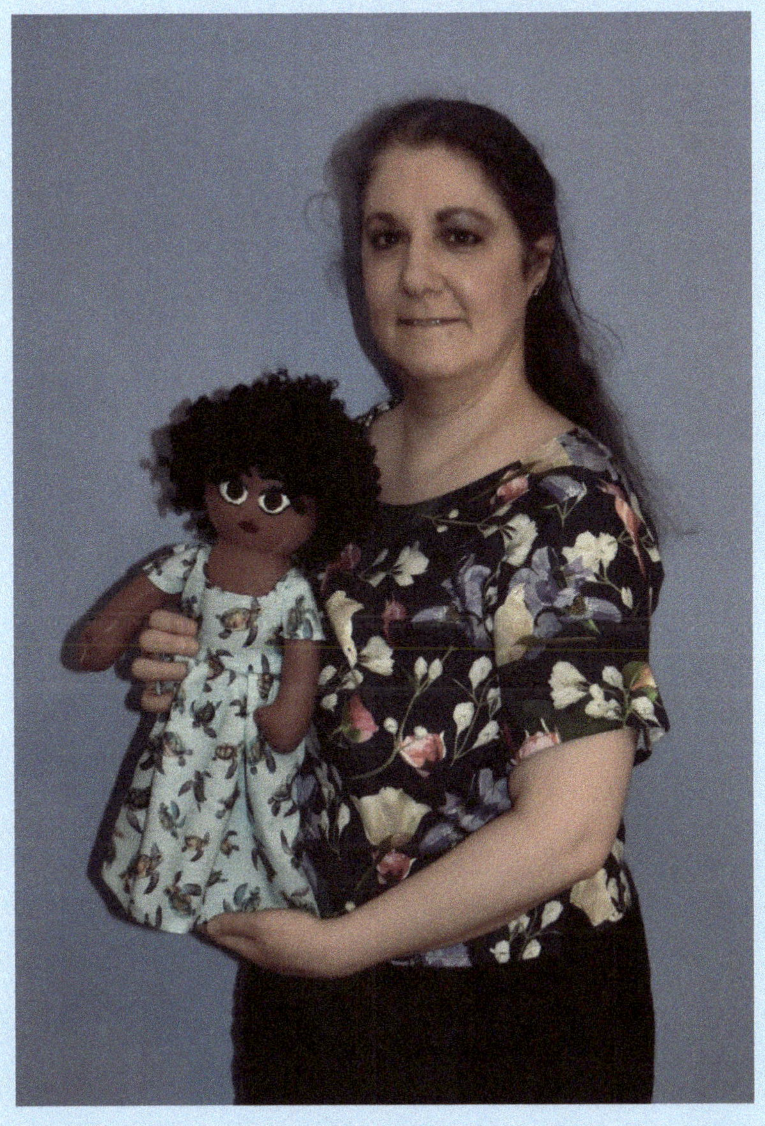

Willow and Stephanie

Legal Assistance for Reproductive Freedom

If you are a woman of reproductive age and need to access abortion health care, and you live in a state that seeks to deny you the legal right to access it, there are attorneys who will help you.

If/When/How is a group of attorneys who have made it their mission to do just that:

If/When/How
Lawyering for Reproductive Justice
https://ifwhenhow.org/

Repro Legal Helpline: 844-868-2812
www.reprolegalhelpline.org
Do you have questions about abortion laws in your state?
Have the police contacted you about an abortion?
Are you being denied an emergency abortion?
Do you need a lawyer for a judicial bypass hearing?
Have you been harmed during labor or birth?

Repro Legal Defense Fund: 866-463-RLDF
www.reprolegaldefensefund.org
Do you need funding for bail or legal fees for your criminal, family, or immigration defense?
Do you represent someone criminalized for abortion or their pregnancy outcome?

Source Material

1. Jessica Valenti writes a blog and newsletter called **Abortion, Every Day**. It is full of news reports and the consequences of blocking abortion care access. Link: https://jessica.substack.com/

2. Kavitha Surana and Lizzie Presser with Lexi Parra, ""Ticking Time Bomb": A Pregnant Mother Kept Getting Sicker. She Died After She Couldn't Get an Abortion in Texas," *ProPublica*, November 19, 2025, Link: https://www.propublica.org/article/texas-abortion-ban-tierra-walker-preeclampsia

3. Rachel Treisman, "A stock of U.S.-bought birth control, meant for sub-Saharan Africa, goes bad in Belgium," *NPR — Goats and Soda*, November 15, 2025, https://www.npr.org/sections/goats-and-soda/2025/11/15/g-s1-97843/birth-control-contraceptives-usaid-belgium-unusable-storage

4. Stephanie Nolen, Jeanna Smialek, and Edward Wong, "$10 Million in Contraceptives Have Been Destroyed on Orders from Trump Officials," *The New York Times*, September 11, 2025, https://www.nytimes.com/2025/09/11/health/usaid-contraceptives-destroyed-trump.html

5. Jeanna Smialek and Stephanie Nolen, "As Trump Administration Plans to Burn Contraceptives, Europeans Are Alarmed," *The New York Times*, August 7, 2025, https://www.nytimes.com/2025/08/07/world/europe/usaid-contraceptives-trump.html

6. Alexis Sterling, "Trump administration to burn $10 million in contraceptives meant for global aid," *Nation of Change*, July 30, 2025, https://www.nationofchange.org/2025/07/30/trump-administration-to-burn-10-million-in-contraceptives-meant-for-global-aid/

7. Rachel Wells, "Pregnant Woman in Tennessee Denied Care for Being Unmarried: The 2025 Medical Ethics Defense Act allows physicians to deny care to patients whose "lifestyles" they disagree with," *TN Repro News*, July 18, 2025, https://wellsrachelm.substack.com/p/pregnant-woman-in-tennessee-denied

8. Katia Riddle, "California bill would protect doctors who mail abortion medication to patients," NPR *Morning Edition*, July 7, 2025, https://www.npr.org/2025/07/07/nx-s1-5452449/california-bill-would-protect-doctors-who-mail-abortion-medication-to-patients

9. KFF (Kaiser Family Foundation), "State Shield Laws: Protections for Abortion and Gender-

Affirming Care Providers," as of 2025,
https://www.kff.org/womens-health-
policy/state-indicator/shield-laws/

10. Senator Alex Padilla, Democrat of California:
Letter to Scott Matheson, Superintendent of
Documents for the U.S. Government Publishing
Office, designating the Internet Archive as a
federal depository library in California, July 24,
2025, https://archive.org/details/padilla-
designation-letter-to-gpo-7.24.2025

11. Chris Freeland, "Internet Archive Designated as
a Federal Depository Library," July 24, 2025,
Federal Depository Library Program,
https://blog.archive.org/2025/07/24/internet-
archive-designated-as-a-federal-depository-
library/

12. Pam Belluck, "F.D.A. Approves a New Generic
Abortion Pill," *The New York Times*, October 2,
2025,
https://www.nytimes.com/2025/10/02/health/
abortion-pill-generic-fda.html

About the Author

Stephanie C. Fox, J.D. is a historian, writer, and editor. She is a graduate of William Smith College and of the University of Connecticut School of Law.

She runs an editing service called **QueenBeeEdit**, which caters to politicians, scientists, and others, which can be accessed at https://www.queenbeeedit.com.

Her imprint is **QueenBeeBooks**. Her shop on Etsy, for doll clothing, is **QueenBeeCouturière**, found at https://queenbeecouturiere.etsy.com

Stephanie lives in Connecticut, and has written books about a variety of topics, including Asperger's, the global financial meltdown, honey bee colony collapse disorder, travelogues of trips to Kuwait and Hawai'i, the effects of human overpopulation on the environment, and cats.